Technology:

A Ticking Time Bomb

Aarkan Singhal

Contents

CHAPTER

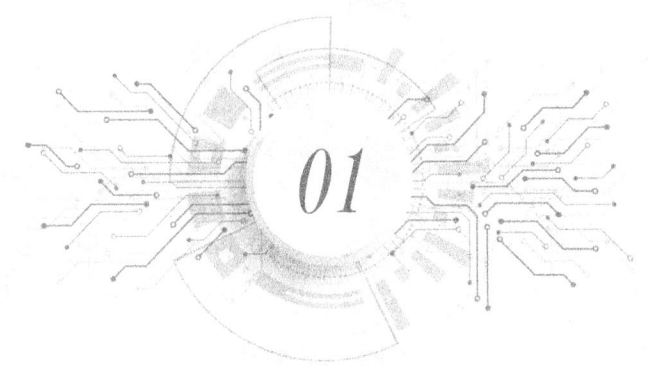

01

T he year was 2130.

The evening sun cast a golden glow across the neighborhood, reflecting off sleek glass walls that shimmered like water. People glided by silently on hoverboards, their post-work routines unfolding in the quiet streets. Towering homes rose three, sometimes four stories high, their smooth, mirrored surfaces absorbing the light and flickering with embedded digital panels. Some windows displayed soft holographic art drifting lazily, while others streamed scrolling news feeds visible only to their owners. Along the curbs, humanoid figures moved in a steady, programmed rhythm, sweeping debris into hovering waste collectors.

Though these figures looked human, they were not. They shared the same height and identical tanned skin. Each wore black pants and a white t-shirt stamped with a badge on the left side that read *Street Sweeper*. Their eyes blinked every ten seconds. Some moved faster than humanly possible, zipping past in a blur, while others crept along at a sluggish pace. The difference was easy to spot—newer models, fresh from the factory, gleamed as they worked with machine-like precision. The older units, dulled by years of use, strained with every movement, their joints stiff and hesitant.

As the street sweepers carried out their programmed tasks, a few vehicles peeled away from traffic and glided into the glass neighborhood. Drivers parked in their driveways, stepping out with briefcases in hand, which they promptly passed off to the human-like figures emerging from their homes.

One car turned onto this very street. It was a vehicle of such pure, polished silver that it seemed to slice through the road. The car bolted forward, not unlike a streak of lightning, until it reached a cul-de-sac marked by a green sign that read *1578 to 1582 Rubik's Street*. There, the car pivoted gracefully and came to a stop in front of a two-story house with elegant glass windows and a front porch made of pristine marble, all crowned by a pair of fashionable glass doors etched with the number *1582* in gold lettering.

The left-side door opened, and a man stepped out. Instantly, a hoverboard appeared on the sidewalk. He climbed onto it and glided toward the house while the car quietly rolled away, disappearing down the street.

The man wore a suit and tie. He appeared to be in his mid-twenties, with dark brown eyes, jet-black hair, and pale skin. A brown briefcase dangled from one hand, and a badge on his suit jacket read *Eric Johansen, CTO.*

The hoverboard came to a stop at the front porch dais. Eric stepped down and approached the door. A pair of blue robotic arms emerged, deftly untying his shoes, while another pair placed cold metallic fingers against the heels. Eric barely noticed. It was just another ordinary evening—coming home after a long day spent writing code, planning projects for better robots, and enduring yet another string of dull office meetings.

The door opened, and a male voice with an Australian accent said, "Welcome home, Eric Johansen."

Eric entered the house in his socks as the porch tiles whisked his shoes away.

From there, Eric climbed the flight of stairs and crossed his bedroom to enter his walk-in closet. The walls were lined with robotic arms, each designed for a specific purpose. One arm was programmed to remove his shirt, and another to take off his belt. The racks, drawers, cabinets, and hangers held shirts, coats, jackets, pants, underthings, belts, and pajamas. The moment he stepped inside, the robotic arms activated. One grabbed his briefcase and badge and set them just outside the room. Next, they removed Eric's belt and placed it in an aqua-colored basket. They stripped him of his pants, jacket, shirt, and socks, folding the garments neatly into a pile.

Then, the arms dressed Eric in a pair of blue shorts and a black t-shirt that read *TechStars*. Once properly attired, Eric left the closet and moved to the living room.

Three teal couches surrounded a coffee table, and four glass walls—hologram screens when activated—displayed an array of tabs. On the left screen, a list of reminders appeared alongside a search bar with results for *how to write Fordo Programming Language*. On the front screen, a calendar displayed events like *the April 5th meeting with Anand Agrawal and the April 24th board of directors meeting*. A shopping list hovered beside the reminders, along with tabs showing the weather and the diagnosis of a prototype robot.

On the right screen, a large digital clock displayed the time. Six light bulbs hung from the ceiling, casting a soft, yellow-toned light.

Eric settled into the cushions and waved his hand. Instantly, the tabs on the hologram screens vanished, replaced by an animation of a sandy beach. A sense of serenity began to wash over him as he listened to the seagulls soaring overhead and the rhythmic crash of waves against the shore. It was as though all the negativity drained from his body, replaced by peacefulness and calm. The feeling crept toward his tired mind, leaving him with the simple desire to sink into the couch and stay there forever.

From his reclined position, Eric said, "Bank, is my dinner ready yet?"

The Australian male voice replied, "It will be ready in twelve minutes. It is spaghetti and meatballs, just like you requested. In the meantime, would you like another theme?"

"Hmm, how about a forest background? I haven't tried that one yet."

"Very well."

The scene shifted to a swampy rainforest. Though the hypnotic sense of comfort never left him, the sounds changed to rustling trees, singing birds, and the steady patter of raindrops.

Eric was overwhelmed by the sight—it was as if he were standing in a real rainforest. He'd seen live trees before, but none like these. They gleamed in the dim sunlight, water dripping from their leaves. He had never witnessed anything so vivid. He was sure he could touch them.

Just a few more steps.

He was close. He knew it was real.

Four.

The birds grew louder; he could hear the parakeet calling again.

Three.

Flowers bloomed around the trees, perfuming the air with their aroma.

Two.

He was so close—he could feel it.

One.

He was there. Now, all he had to do was reach.

Reach.

Reach for the bark of the tree.

The moment Eric stretched out his hand to touch the tree, it vanished—and a diagnostic of a prototype robot took its place.

Eric blinked, dazed. No, he wasn't in a rainforest. He was in his living room, his right hand pressed against the wall. Sullenly, he returned to the couch and sat back down—perhaps a little too hard, as a faint creaking noise echoed at that precise moment. The beach theme played on the screens once more, but Eric was too disappointed by what had just happened to let the program soothe him.

A few minutes later, Bank's voice announced, "Sir, your dinner is ready. It is in the dining area."

Eric wandered into the dining room, which was similar to the living room. Three hologram screens surrounded a table with six seats. A plate of spaghetti sat near the head of the table.

He sat down and took a bite of his spaghetti. The disappointment from the living room faded as he savored the rich marinara sauce, the tender pasta perfectly mixed with luscious meatballs. The flavors were familiar, comforting in a world where so little felt real anymore.

As he continued eating, Bank asked, "Would you like to watch some television, sir?"

"Sure," Eric replied. "How about Bot News? That should be sufficient."

"Yes, sir. Playing Bot News now."

A tab on the wall opposite Eric expanded, revealing the news channel. A female reporter appeared on screen, speaking about a tragic event from earlier that day.

An icon on the left read *Bot News,* while a banner scrolled across the bottom: *Breaking News: Condo Building Fire on Skyline Street.* The reporter was beautiful, with almond-shaped eyes, golden hair, and caramel skin. But Eric wasn't fooled—she was a robot, just like all the others. Robots reported the news now, not humans.

"This is Mary 5000, reporting on the condo fire on Skyline Street. More details are underway, but let's get to the facts. Detectives are still investigating how the fire started, but thanks to our firefighter robots, the blaze was extinguished shortly after it ignited. There were no fatalities, but five people suffered minor injuries. Here is the recorded footage."

The screen shifted to a video of a towering 25-story condo building.

Flames burst from a high window, licking at the sky. Within moments, a fire truck arrived on the scene. Five robots spilled onto the street. They had dark skin, red pants, and red T-shirts stamped with Firefighters' badges. One grabbed the hose while another manned the controls. Water gushed out in powerful streams as the robots directed it toward the upper floors.

Three of the firefighting units ignited thrusters on their backs and soared toward the roof, disappearing into the smoke as they began the rescue.

As the flames were beaten back, five ambulances pulled up. Ten robots—two from each ambulance—climbed out. Their uniforms matched the firefighters' style but were pure white, with *Paramedic* badges gleaming on their chests. Each pair retrieved a stretcher from their vehicle and flew straight to the rooftop. Within seconds, they returned carrying injured humans, laying them carefully on the stretchers before activating the sirens. The ambulances took off toward the nearest hospital.

Eric exhaled, his gaze fixed on the screen, watching as the firefighter robots subdued the last of the blaze. They flew down from the rooftop, wound up the hose with precision, climbed back into the fire truck, and drove off like it was just another job.

Moments later, a police car arrived. Two robots dressed in black stepped out from the front. Without hesitation, they moved to the back and opened the door. Two men in suits and ties emerged—detectives, by the look of them—and followed the police units into the damaged building. The video clip ended.

The reporter returned to the screen. "As you can see, the fire was quickly managed. The five victims have been treated and are expected to make a full recovery. A construction crew has patched the damage, so the building is structurally sound, and those affected will return to their homes as soon as possible."

She paused slightly, her artificial tone shifting as if programmed for concern. "Detectives believe the fire was caused by faulty wiring or possible foul play. Though we don't know for sure, answers are coming soon. We'll be back with more information after the break. Once again, this is Mary 5000 with *Bot News.*"

Music played as the *Bot News* logo appeared on the screen.

"Bank, turn off the channel," Eric said, his appetite fading.

"Yes, sir."

The news tab vanished, leaving the room quiet once more as Eric finished the last bite of his spaghetti. He was about to stand when Bank's voice chimed in again, "May I remind you of your important events?"

"Sure, thanks for the reminder. What do I have?"

"You have a meeting with a team of NASA engineers this Sunday to discuss rocket prototype improvements. You also need to inspect a newly opened plant on Scraper Drive. And you'd better not forget your board of directors meeting next Wednesday."

Eric sighed. "Anything tomorrow?"

"Apparently, you have the day off tomorrow."

A flicker of relief crossed his face. "Good. Make sure to give me reminders tomorrow morning."

"Will do, sir."

Eric pushed back from the table and made his way upstairs, retracing his steps toward the bedroom. The house was expansive, with wide, open hallways and polished marble floors that gleamed beneath the soft yellow lights. His bedroom sat at the end of the second-floor corridor, its entrance flanked by glass panels shimmering faintly with inactive holograms.

Inside, the familiar walk-in closet waited—lined with robotic arms, each poised for its next task.

The blue arms activated the moment he stepped inside. They swiftly removed his shorts, replacing them with loose-fitting pajamas. His shirt was exchanged for a soft nightshirt, the fabric cool against his skin.

Eric returned to his bedroom. The four walls surrounding him were hologram screens, still glowing faintly with the same tabs from the living room. A perfectly made queen-sized bed rested at the center against the back wall.

Without a word, Eric slipped under the covers. As he settled in, the lights dimmed automatically, and Bank's voice sounded one final time.

"Alarm set for seven o'clock, sir. Good night."

Eric closed his eyes, sinking into the bed's comfort as sleep finally claimed him.

CHAPTER

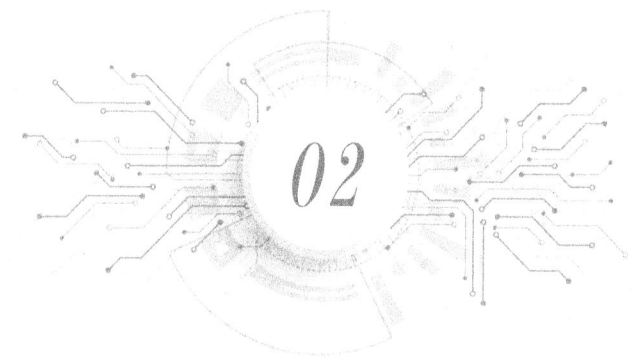

02

A t seven the next day, music filled the room, and Eric opened his eyes.

"It's time to wake up, Mr. Johansen," said Bank.

"Well, Bank, what do I have today?" Eric asked as he sat up.

"You've got the day off from work, but you need to get some groceries. You are out of milk, butter, cheese, bread, watermelon, and pasta. I've added these items to your shopping list. If you don't wish to go to the store, I can send a courier."

"You might as well send a courier, Bank. I was planning to go for a walk in the park this morning."

"Okay, then. I will prepare a portable hoverboard for you to carry along for your ride when it arrives."

"When it gets here, remind me to pick up my tablet and communicator."

"Will do, sir."

Eric swung his feet off the bed and made his way to the bathroom. Every surface gleamed, crafted from clear marble, except for the hologram screen that doubled as a mirror. He opened the restroom door, closed it behind him, and relieved himself. When he came out, a small robotic arm popped out of the wall and automatically brushed his teeth.

He spit out the remaining paste, washed his hands, and headed into the walk-in closet. This time, the robotic arms dressed him in jeans and a blue t-shirt.

Eric went downstairs for breakfast. When he entered the dining room, he found a stack of buttermilk pancakes waiting for him, accompanied by a side of scrambled eggs. He sat down, picked up the knife and fork neatly placed on either side of the plate, and dug in.

The wall in front of him lit up with several tabs as Bank's voice filled the room. "Sir, the temperature today is eighty-one degrees Fahrenheit." A tab displaying the weather drifted across the wall. "The high is eighty-four degrees, and the low is seventy-nine degrees. Judging by my calculations, the best clothing to wear would be something lighter since we have such warm weather today."

A small grimace crossed Eric's lips. The weather couldn't have been better for a walk.

Bank continued, "Now, reminders from work." Eric shifted in his seat as the tabs rearranged on the screen. "You are supposed to receive an analysis of a new computing chip from Jane Kessel. The chip is rumored to contain at least two thousand transistors. However, it needs review before it can be used in the robots."

"Yeah, about that, Bank," Eric interrupted. "Tell Amy to remind me to discuss the matter with Jane on Tuesday. We need that prototype ready, and I believe it requires modifications. Jamal said multiple companies have placed massive orders for these chips to be delivered at the end of May."

Bank replied, "CEO Jamal Rao is correct. I will send a message to Amy to set the reminders on that matter. In the meantime, here is the latest on the news."

Eric returned to his breakfast as Bank began reciting the headlines. A new tab appeared on the wall, displaying the news page.

"There were no further injuries from the condo fire on Skyline Street yesterday, and those with minor injuries are back at work. However, detectives investigating the case determined the cause of the fire was a weak, intense heat absorber. A construction crew has installed a new absorber, so the matter is now settled."

Eric toyed with his fork, half-listening as Bank continued.

"President Brandt Costello signed a new bill that allows malfunctioning or dilapidated robots to be disassembled for parts and repurposed for new robots. This bill received a majority vote in the Senate and the House of Representatives. It's expected to save tons of waste aluminum, iron, and other materials. Here is what the president said when he addressed his cabinet this morning:"

A clip of an office meeting—apparently the President's cabinet—flashed onto the screen. The President sat at the head of the table with a folder in front of him. He wore a suit and blue tie. His caramel-toned skin wasn't too wrinkled yet, but signs of age had begun to show. His black hair was streaked with white, though his dark brown eyes remained sharp.

"I, President Brandt Costello, hereby announce that the Conservative Material Act of 2130 will soon take effect," the man said onscreen. "This act will allow waste material to serve another great purpose. Hundreds of people worldwide have been suffering from our waste products, but today, their misery shall be no more.

"Another piece of legislation is underway to extract more waste material from our wastelands. The House of Representatives will debate it tomorrow morning.

"As nations and as people, we are not always perfect. Mistakes have been made by all of us—and by our ancestors. Right now, we are on track to correct one grave mistake. This is the beginning of a bright future for our country, our people, and our planet."

Applause filled the room, and the clip ended.

Immediately, Eric was plunged into the past. All he knew was that he saw something—no, someone—in front of him.

He was five, standing before the glass wall in his bedroom, trying to imitate someone giving a speech. "I, President Eric Johansen—"

"Eric?"

His mom opened the door.

"Sweetie, were you play-acting again?"

Eric could see himself nodding to his mother.

"What were you pretending to be?"

"The president," he answered brightly. "When I take office, I'll rule the country and make people do what I want."

His mother chuckled. "Honey, there's more to being president than what you think. Let's talk about it at dinner."

"What's for dinner?" he asked eagerly.

"Cheese pizza with apple pie for dessert. But you'd better come down quickly, or else the big hungry bear will take it away." She snarled playfully like an angry bear, and Eric grinned.

"Okay, Mommy."

Eric snapped out of the memory as two tears streamed down his cheeks. He often missed the comfort of family around him. After attaining such a high position at such a young age, there was always a heavy workload tagging along, leaving him with only rare days off like today.

He wiped his cheeks and took a steadying breath, pushing the memory aside. There was no time to dwell—not today.

Eric finished his breakfast and stood to leave, needing the fresh air. But just as he took a few steps, Bank's voice stopped him.

"Wait, sir."

Eric responded reluctantly, "What, Bank?"

"Remember to bring your tablet and communicator. And I have booked a car to take you to the park."

Eric blinked. "Oh, right. Thanks for the reminder."

He jogged upstairs, tucked his communicator into his pocket, and grabbed his tablet before heading out to the front porch.

Robotic arms reached out to put on his socks, and his sneakers appeared atop two tiles. Eric slid his feet into the shoes, and the robotic hands automatically tied them.

A hoverboard appeared, and Eric stepped onto it, letting it carry him down to the sidewalk.

A car drove into the cul-de-sac and opened its door. Eric paused, realizing Bank must have booked it despite his plan to walk. With a sigh, he stepped inside and found a comfortable sofa with a rack on the right side. He placed his shoes on the rack and set his communication device on top of them. Eric sat back as the door closed, and the car drove off.

He stared out the window, watching as cars zoomed down the street and trees passed by in a blur. Somehow, seeing it all made him feel at home. It was a simple pleasure to cruise along and take in the beautiful sights. After a while, the car stopped in front of a park with a sign that read *Villa Park: Where Beauty Has a Name.* The left-side door opened. Eric slipped his shoes back on, tucked his communicator into his pocket, and kept his tablet in hand as he stepped outside.

As the car drove off to find a parking spot, Eric walked a winding path through the greenery. Dozens of trees were scattered about, but most of the park was covered in lush grass. The idyllic setting was perfect for picnics, but Eric continued on.

He paused near a playground enclosed within a magnificent glass dome and watched as children played tag. Artificial Intelligence bots monitored the scene from inside the dome, allowing parents to relax elsewhere in the park. One called out, "Johnny, it is time for you to go home." Another said, "Watch your step, Grace. You don't want your mother fussing over you."

Eric strolled onward. The weather was perfect—the slight breeze, the children's laughter, the trees giving fresh oxygen—it felt good to be in this environment where everything was so calm and cool. It was like being at home, but better.

When Eric reached a VR fountain, he took a seat on one of the empty benches surrounding it. The water feature wasn't ordinary—it contained a virtual environment that could change based on the user's commands, turning simple water into anything from animals to landscapes.

Eric decided he'd walked enough. He'd rest here for a while, then head back to the car and finish sightseeing.

Turning on his tablet, he opened the app that linked directly to his AI system. "Bank, change the theme of the fountain to birds."

"Yes, sir."

Within seconds, birds appeared around the fountain—sparrows, finches, and robins—flitting across the water's surface, pecking at the ground and feeding their young. The holograms were so detailed that, for a moment, Eric forgot what he'd asked for.

"Hey, Bank... are these real birds?"

"No, sir. These are fully rendered holographic projections. Wildlife photographers captured images and videos of real birds performing these exact actions."

Eric stared, still taken aback by how lifelike they appeared. "No, I mean... are they actually here?"

"No, sir. The birds are simply part of the VR fountain's display. There are no real animals in the park."

Eric sank back against the bench, his chest tightening with disappointment. It was almost unimaginable that this was just a program. The color of their feathers, the shape of their beaks, the soft rustle of their wings—it all looked so real. For a moment, it had felt as if the birds belonged here, living among the trees and grass.

But no—there were no real animals in the park.

A quiet ache crept through him. He wished, not for the first time that he'd learned more about birds when he was younger. Maybe then, he'd know what species they were or understand their behaviors. Instead, all he could do was watch the imitation.

Sighing, Eric opened his tablet again and scrolled through his digital library of books. When he clicked the icon, he found the same titles he'd already read. He needed something new.

"Hey, Bank?"

"Yes?"

"I want to buy a new book. Could you give some suggestions?"

"Hmm... let's see. What kind of book would you like to read?"

"Well, anything. But if you want my preference, maybe something written in the 19th century."

"There is *The Adventures of Tom Sawyer* by Mark Twain, one of the greatest authors of his time."

"Okay, how much does it cost?"

"$13.99."

"Make the purchase with my credit card."

A few minutes later, the book appeared on Eric's reading list. He tapped on the cover and began to read.

CHAPTER

03

M usic filled the room, and Eric opened his eyes. Another day had begun.

"Well, Bank, what do I have today?" he asked groggily.

"You need to get to the office and review the chip prototype with Jane Kessel and Matt Ignitus. Jamal Rao has already arrived and will be joining the meeting."

"All right, looks like it's going to be a busy day."

"It is indeed," Bank replied. "You also need to prepare for the board of directors meeting."

"Oh, great. That boring thing."

"Boring? You marked that as *very important* in your calendar."

"Bank, you know what I mean."

Eric swung his feet over the side of the bed and headed for the bathroom. After relieving himself, he brushed his teeth, washed his hands, and spat out the extra paste. The cold marble gleamed under the lights, and the quiet hum of the automated systems filled the air.

He stepped into the closet, where the robotic arms awaited him. They dressed him quickly—fresh undergarments, black pants, and a crisp blue shirt tucked in and buttoned. The arms secured his fly, tied a single Windsor knot around his neck, and straightened the tie before fastening the collar buttons. A belt slid into place, followed by his socks and jacket. Finally, one of the arms clipped his badge onto his chest pocket. It read: *Eric Johansen, CTO.*

Grabbing his briefcase, Eric opened the front door. Shiny black shoes appeared on the porch, and he slipped them on. A hoverboard glided forward, and Eric stepped on, allowing it to carry him smoothly to the waiting car. He dismounted with practiced ease and entered from the left side.

The car interior was designed for business—two rows of forward-facing seats instead of the usual couch. Eric sat in the front left seat and placed his briefcase on the right.

Once the door closed, the car pulled away. Eric leaned back, letting the smooth motion settle him as his thoughts shifted to the chip prototype. Everything depended on it working.

The car took several turns through the city, passing tall, gleaming towers and sweeping views of the skyline before pulling up to a sleek blue skyscraper with *Nanocom* emblazoned in sleek metallic lettering across the front. Eric climbed out, picked up his briefcase, and made his way inside as the car disappeared back into traffic.

The lobby's polished stone floors reflected the morning light like liquid glass. Eric passed the front desk, where a young receptionist glanced up with a polite, practiced smile—eyes tired but professional. Eric nodded in return and continued toward the glass doors ahead.

Beyond them, a transparent elevator box waited. As Eric approached, the doors slid open with a soft hiss and a familiar voice greeted him. "Good morning, Eric Johansen. Please step inside."

Eric entered the glass-walled elevator, and the doors closed seamlessly behind him. The elevator began its smooth ascent, the city falling away below.

Moments later, it slowed to a stop before another set of glass doors. The voice returned, crisp and efficient. "Level thirty-five. Offices for the CEO, COO, CFO, CIO, CTO, CDO, CMO, and CSO. Please step out."

Eric stepped into the wide, carpeted hallway and walked past the offices of his colleagues. He paused when he reached the door that read: *Office of Eric Johansen, Chief Technology Officer*.

The door swung open automatically, and Eric stepped inside. The room was expansive—two hologram walls displayed streams of data and design specs, while two smaller panels flanked the door behind him. A large window at the back of the room allowed natural light to flood the space.

To the right, a spacious sitting area held a large couch, two armchairs, and a coffee table. To the left, a conference table stood ready. At the center, perfectly positioned before the window, sat a dark brown desk with a compact holographic computer hovering above it and a comfortable office chair waiting.

Eric closed the door behind him and walked to the desk. He placed his briefcase beside the chair, pulled out his sleek silver laptop, and set it carefully on the surface. As he settled in, a female voice with a smooth American accent greeted him. "Good morning, Eric."

"Good morning, Amy," he replied.

Amy, his AI assistant, responded as the holographic interface blinked to life above the desk. A virtual keyboard and touchpad materialized, suspended mid-air. Eric leaned forward, tapping and swiping through several data streams as he settled into his morning routine.

"You've just received an email from Matt Ignitus," Amy informed him. "Shall I display it?"

"Sure," Eric said. "Put it through my desk holoscreen."

"Very well."

An email appeared, hovering in front of him. Eric scanned it quickly, frowning slightly. "Amy, when do I have my meeting with Jane, Matt, and Jamal?"

"The meeting is scheduled for noon. It will take at least an hour."

"Okay. In the meantime, tell Jane to make sure she has the analysis ready before the meeting. If we don't get that chip finalized before the deadline, our stock will take a heavy hit. Speaking of which, make a voice call on the company frequency to the CDO—whoever it is."

"Yes, sir. Calling Jason Wang now."

Eric continued typing as the system connected the call.

A moment later, a voice came through. "Hello?"

"Hey, Jason, it's Eric. I wanted to check—has our stock price dropped, or are we holding steady at this stage?"

"That's a good question, Eric," Jason replied. "One of my data analysts just reported a rise. It could increase even more with the purchase of the product we're preparing to sell. I understand you're working on the new chip?"

"Yeah, my hardware developers are on it."

"Well, if it performs, we're looking at a major boost in profits. The chip's testing better than the last model so far. I'm sure it'll—"

"I know, I know," Eric cut in. "Just tell me—will this improve our standing?"

"As I said, yes. Absolutely."

"Good. Tell your analysts to send me copies of the recorded data—just for reference."

"Will do. Thanks for the call."

"My pleasure."

The call ended, and Eric hung up, turning his attention back to the email on his screen.

He worked steadily, reviewing specs and calculations until the clock struck eleven. Then he glanced up. "Amy, what time is my meeting today?"

"It was moved to 12:15," she replied.

Eric glanced at the holoscreen. "And the time now?"

"Eleven-oh-one."

Eric sighed. "Fine. I guess I'll get some lunch."

"What would you like?" Amy asked.

"Four slices of cheese pizza, personal size."

"Okay. I'm ordering your pizza. It should arrive in about twenty-five minutes," Amy confirmed.

"Perfect. I'll take a walk while I wait."

Eric stood, grabbed his jacket, and left his office. He took the elevator down, and as it stopped, the familiar voice announced, "Level one—lobby and front desk. Please step out."

Outside, Eric found an empty bench nestled near the landscaping. He stretched out, watching the slow parade of cars along the road. The quiet was a welcome change. For once, there was nothing demanding his attention—no screens, no alerts—just the steady rhythm of the world moving around him.

He took a long breath, letting his eyes linger on the greenery and the clean lines of the building. Everything had been designed to encourage moments like this, but no one ever seemed to stop. Except now, he did.

For a while, he stayed there—stretching his arms, rolling his shoulders, letting his mind drift somewhere quiet. It had been a long time since something as simple as fresh air felt like a luxury.

Eventually, Eric stood and made his way back inside. By the time he returned to his office, the pizza was waiting on the couch. He sat down, opened the box, and took his first bite. The pizza was still hot, fresh from the oven, and the cheese perfectly melted. The taste hit him harder than he expected—a small, satisfying reminder that there were still simple things left to enjoy.

For a moment, everything else faded, and he let himself savor it.

When he was finished, Eric sat back down at his desk and continued working until Amy's voice broke through. "Sir, Matt Ignitus, Jane Kessel, and Jamal Rao are at your door."

"Let them in, Amy. I just need to complete this email."

The door opened, revealing the trio.

Matt Ignitus stepped in first, dressed casually in a fitted blue shirt and dark jeans, his sleeves rolled up as if he'd come straight from the lab. Jamal Rao followed, crisp in a charcoal suit and tie, his polished shoes silent on the floor. Jane Kessel came last, her tailored pink dress striking against the muted tones of the room, every inch of her composed and professional. They greeted Eric and took their seats at the conference table. Eric brought his laptop and settled at the head.

"Good afternoon," Eric began. "I called this meeting because a new chip with powerful capabilities has been designed at our factory. It's expected to make our robots faster and more agile. I spoke with the CDO, Jason Wang, and his analysts sent me some preliminary data. Amy, bring it up."

The data appeared across the table's surface, and all four leaned in to study it.

"As you can see," Eric continued, "this product could be a significant asset to the company. But we need to confirm the chip's reliability. Jane, you've already analyzed it. The floor is yours."

Jane gave a slight nod. "Thank you, Eric. While it may need a few modifications, the chip has worked beautifully with our robots. Amy, bring up file AN19."

A hologram of the chip materialized above the table. Eric tapped the desk, setting the three-dimensional sketch slowly spinning.

Jamal leaned forward, adjusting his cufflinks. "Jane, do you really believe this can work?"

"I do," Jane replied, her voice steady. "My team's run it through multiple tests. So far, it's performed perfectly."

"Can you pull up the test results?" Jamal asked.

"Of course. Amy, display the AN19 test results."

The hologram shifted, streams of data scrolling through the air. Jamal reviewed the figures, his expression thoughtful. Finally, he nodded. "All right. You have my approval to continue. Matt, any thoughts?"

Matt, who'd been silent until now, leaned forward. "It looks solid. But maybe we should examine the internal structure a bit closer. Amy, widen the chip and provide marking pens."

Silver pens appeared on the table as the chip hologram expanded, revealing intricate layers.

For the next few hours, they worked—marking key areas, debating potential weaknesses, and refining their analysis. By the end, the team seemed satisfied. One by one, they thanked Eric and returned to their departments.

Eric stayed behind, typing steadily until the clock struck six.

"Sir," Amy chimed, "it is time for you to leave. Traffic is getting worse, and it's best to start now if you want to reach home by seven."

Eric minimized the report he'd been reading and nodded. "Okay, Amy. Book a car."

"Already done. Would you like me to arrange dinner?"

"Tomato soup will do tonight. I'm feeling pretty full."

"And a reminder—tomorrow is Saturday. You can work from home."

"Perfect. Thanks, Amy."

"You're welcome."

Eric left his office and took the elevator to the lobby. A sleek company car, its doors already open, was waiting at the curb. He climbed into the front seat, and the car pulled away smoothly. Almost immediately, Eric noticed the route was different—no traffic, no congestion.

Amy must have programmed an alternate route.

The city blurred past, glass buildings fading into distant mountains until the car reached Rubik's Street. It turned neatly into the cul-de-sac and slowed to a stop. Eric grabbed his briefcase just as a hoverboard appeared, gliding him the final stretch to the front porch while the car disappeared silently down the road. His shoes were untied as the door opened, and Banks greeted him. "Welcome home, Eric Johansen."

Eric stepped inside, too drained to change out of his clothes. The day had been long. He sank into the couch as the familiar beach theme played softly through the house.

Tomorrow, he reminded himself that he still had that meeting with the NASA engineers. So much for a quiet Saturday.

CHAPTER

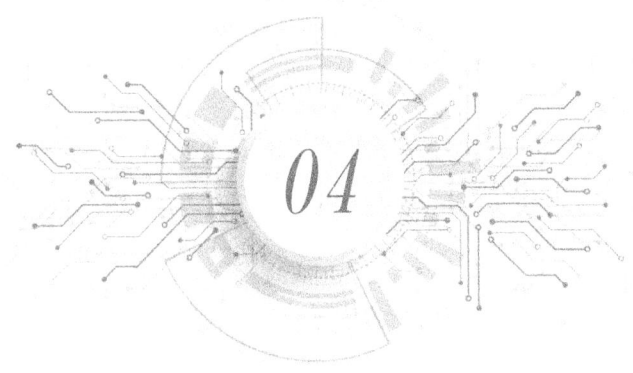

04

A nother day began in the sprawling city where technology thrived, as Eric sat in the dining area, eating his breakfast. He slowly shoveled his food into his mouth, tapping his fork on the plate between bites.

Tap. Tap. Tap.

Eric couldn't focus. The memory—and everything it dragged back with it—kept circling his mind.

Tap. Tap. Tap.

He'd barely slept the night before. Restless, staring at the ceiling, haunted by that memory... and worse, by the looming pressure of the chip modifications. For the first time, Eric couldn't find peace—not even in sleep. He'd been troubled before, but never like this.

Tap. Tap. Tap.

The worst-case scenarios played out in his head, over and over. Not even a calming theme helped this time.

Tap. Tap. Tap.

The chip needed dozens of modifications. If he didn't fix them, he'd miss the deadline.

Tap. Tap. Tap.

If he missed the deadline, the consumers would back out.

Tap. Tap. Tap.

If they canceled their orders, Nanocom's stock would fall.

Tap. Tap. Tap.

If the stock price dropped, shareholders would sell. The company would spiral.

Tap. Tap. Tap.

Nanocom could suffer massive losses. Maybe even fail.

Tap. Tap. Tap.

Bankruptcy.

Tap. Tap. Tap.

Bad press.

Tap. Tap. Tap.

Layoffs.

Tap. Tap. Tap.

He'd lose his job.

Tap. Tap. Tap.

And then what? What company would take him after that?

Tap. Tap. CRASH!

Eric hurled his fork across the room. It clattered against the wall—nothing broke, but the sound echoed through the house like a gunshot.

Eric huffed and puffed, sweat trickling down his neck. He'd worked his way up so far—CTO at twenty-six—and couldn't bear the thought of starting over. Jamal Rao had even told him that if he stepped down, Eric could be next in line for CEO. But if Nanocom went bankrupt… what then? Who would hire him again?

Bank's voice broke through Eric's spiral. "Sir, is something wrong?"

"Yes, Bank. Yes."

"What is it?"

"I'm going to lose my job. Nanocom's going to go bankrupt. I worked so hard to get here… what am I supposed to do now?"

Bank replied gently, "Don't worry—you're going to be okay. You told me Jamal Rao said you might become CEO when he steps down, remember?"

"Yeah… but what happens if the chips aren't ready in time?"

"You'll be okay," Bank reassured him. "Don't focus on the worst-case outcomes. Think about what you *can* control—getting those chips ready. Focus on the modifications and the plan you'll give the manufacturers."

"But what if I fail? I'll have no job, no food, no house, no AI system—nothing."

"Don't worry. I'm always here for you. Make the plan. You'll save Nanocom. But you need some inspiration."

Eric let out a shaky breath. "All right… I'll try. What should I do?"

"You should visit the Museum of Human History. There's an exhibit about humans who lived in the past. I know you're fascinated with history. If I remember correctly… you aced every test in your history classes."

Eric blinked, startled. *How does he know that?* Did Roger—his childhood AI system—transfer his old records to Bank?

The surprise passed quickly. "Where's the museum?"

"It's just a few miles away. I've already booked a car for you. I hope you'll enjoy the visit."

"Okay… I'll get my shoes on."

Eric grabbed his laptop from his briefcase and headed to the front door. His sports shoes appeared, and robotic arms laced them onto his feet. He stepped onto the hoverboard, letting it carry him down to the sidewalk.

Reaching the driveway, Eric climbed into the waiting car, placed his communicator on the shelf, and settled onto the couch.

But instead of enjoying the ride, Eric flipped open his laptop. The holoscreen lit up as he began typing. While the car glided through the streets, Eric buried himself in his project—his mind already working.

Finally, the car arrived at its destination. Eric closed his laptop, leaving it on the couch, and stepped out with his communicator in hand. Instead of picking up another passenger, the vehicle darkened its windows and glided off to find a parking spot.

Eric powered on his communicator, scrolling through the holographic contact list until he found Bank's name. He tapped the icon.

"Hello," Bank answered.

Eric slipped an earpiece into place and said, "Bank, can you tell me where the exhibit is?"

"Of course—but first, check in with the museum."

Eric sighed, pocketed the communicator, and joined the line of people waiting to check in. When it was finally his turn, he provided his information and was waved through the entrance.

As he walked inside, Eric tapped his earpiece. "Bank?"

"Yes, sir?"

"Where's the exhibit?"

"Scanning the museum now."

Eric waited while the AI processed the layout.

"Walk forward and turn left," Bank directed.

Eric followed the instructions.

"Keep going straight. You should see an elevator on your left."

Eric turned and spotted the elevator. He stepped inside.

"The elevator will take you to the third floor," Bank added.

The doors slid shut, and a moment later, they opened on the third floor. Eric stepped out.

"Turn left, then right. Keep walking straight," Bank continued.

Eric moved through the quiet halls, following the directions until Bank's voice spoke again. "The exhibit should be on your right."

Eric stopped and glanced over. He almost laughed when he saw the title displayed at the entrance:

HISTORY OF TECHNOLOGY EXHIBIT

How We Have Evolved in Recent Years

"Bank, you said this was about the evolution of human life."

"It is—sort of," Bank replied.

"It only explains the evolution of technology. I've studied this time and time again."

"Well… maybe look again. You might learn something new."

Feeling a bit let down, Eric stepped inside.

It was interesting, he had to admit—but not what he'd hoped for. He found himself wishing the exhibit included ancient civilizations. What was life like during the Roman Republic? No electricity. No personal AI systems. No cars. Just candles or torches lighting the night.

As he wandered, Eric stopped in front of a model of an old fighter jet. His excitement returned as he tapped the holoscreen beside it. The display brightened with the following description:

P-51 Mustang

The P-51 Mustang was used by the American military during World War II. These fighter planes played a crucial role in bombing missions and aerial battles. They were among the fastest and most advanced aircraft of their time, often serving as escorts for bombers deep into enemy territory.

Eric grinned, his heart racing. Incredible.

He moved on to another display—a bulky, odd-looking machine. Curious, he tapped its holoscreen.

Apple 1

The Apple 1 was the first computer designed by legendary computer scientists Steve Jobs and Steve Wozniak. It was a huge success, and its sleek design and powerful processor made it one of the most popular computers of its time. The Apple 1 helped shape the computers we use today.

Further down, an old compact disc cover caught his eye—**Windows 95** printed boldly across the front. Eric tapped the holoscreen:

Windows 95

Windows 95 was one of Microsoft's first operating systems, designed in 1995. Although it is no match for modern systems, it ushered in a new era—the era of technology. Though not initially well-received, it kicked-started the technological advancements we enjoy today.

Eric let out a small breath. *Maybe Bank was right. There's more to this than I thought.*

Eric admitted to himself that Bank was right—there were plenty of fascinating items to see within the exhibit.

At another display, he spotted a row of funny-looking communicators labeled simply as **phones.** He couldn't help but wonder why they were so large—nearly the size of his own tablet.

Further down, Eric found a section dedicated to old tablets. Some were bulky, others had multiple camera lenses—none capable of capturing anything but grainy images by today's standards.

One tablet in particular caught his eye. It had a simple image of a bitten apple in the center. The label read:

iPad

Eric picked it up. The device was heavier than his own tablet—thick, outdated, but strangely impressive. After a moment, he placed it back on the shelf and decided it was time to head home.

"Bank, call my car."

"Yes, sir."

Eric took the elevator down to the lobby and waited outside until his car arrived. Once it pulled up, he climbed inside, settled onto the couch, and opened his laptop. Accessing his private journal, Eric wrote quietly for the duration of the trip.

When the car finally dropped him off at home, Eric went straight to his room and closed the door behind him.

As the car pulled away into the night, a light bulb in his neighbor's house flickered.

CHAPTER

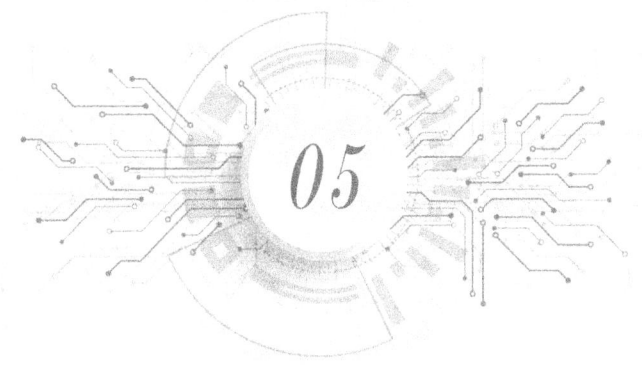

05

F ar from the city, a power plant sat deep within the grasslands. Its steel barriers crackled as they transferred electricity to the city and beyond, powering homes, AI systems, and robots. Above it, toxic white smog billowed from the stacks, clouding the sky.

Power plant management remained one of the few operations still run by humans. It was too risky to hand full control to robots, no matter how advanced. Even with strict safeguards, robots could be hacked and turned into tools for enemy agencies. The plant did contain robots, but they followed limited programming and could only activate on command. They weren't humanoid—just black metal frames with no badges or identifiers.

The facility consisted of two white buildings. One was windowless, where electricity was generated. The other housed the command center, where humans ensured the plant ran at peak efficiency.

Inside the control room, there were no AI systems monitoring operations—just endless rows of switches, buttons, and dials operated by the crew. A specific set of controls featured labeled alarms, topped by a large red glass tube mounted to a metal box on the wall—a last-resort warning system.

Six people manned the command center, all dressed in orange and yellow vests over dirty blue pants. Cassius and Callum sat side by side at the central control desk. Across the room, two others adjusted the energy flow, transforming raw power into usable electricity for the city. Another pair handled the switches. At the far end, a lone worker monitored the system from an aging desktop computer.

Cassius, a heavyset man in his mid-fifties with a long black beard, leaned back in his chair. "What's up with you, Callum?" he asked casually.

"Nothing much," Callum muttered, his voice low. "Just thinking about how bad life is." Thinner than Cassius, though far from slender, deep worry lines creased his forehead.

Cassius clicked a switch, glancing sideways. "What do you mean? My life's great. Hoping to get promoted soon—maybe even move out to the main grid station."

"Good for you, Cassius," Callum scoffed. "But I didn't ask."

The conversation fizzled as they returned to their routine—flicking switches, pressing buttons, eyes half-glazed from the monotony.

"Well," Cassius sighed after a while, "only a couple more hours 'til the next crew takes over."

"Yeah... I'm ready to get home and sleep." Callum yawned. "Wish I was rich like that CFO we saw on TV last night."

"You mean Cynthia Douglas?"

"Yeah. People like her... and that Johansen guy... they've got smart homes, AI systems, hologram walls. Me? I've got an antique tablet that barely runs."

Cassius snorted. "That old thing? When was it made? Back in 2040? It's 2130, man. Time to move on."

"Dude, I can't afford a holoscreen computer. Those things are expensive," Callum muttered, drumming his fingers against the console.

"You're still using a brand that's extinct," Cassius laughed. "I'm shocked you even found a charger."

"I rummaged through an old house for it," Callum admitted. "And yeah, people call me poor, but I live in the mountains. Doesn't bother me."

Cassius grinned. "No offense, but you *are* poor. You don't even have a digicount." He leaned back, arms behind his head.

"I'm not like those rich jerks downtown," Callum shot back, clenching his jaw. He stared at his dusty screen, resentment simmering.

Before Cassius could answer, a sharp voice cut through the air.

"Hey! If you two fat beauties are done gossiping, we've got a power plant to run," Regina snapped. She stood over them, arms crossed, the air of a supervisor who didn't tolerate nonsense.

"Yeah… sorry, Regina," Callum muttered, straightening up and pulling a lever. Cassius smirked but flicked a switch without protest.

Cassius shrugged. "Anyway… get a new computer."

"I'll look into it," Callum sighed. "Still wish I had a CEO's life."

"There's this thing called buying stocks," Cassius teased.

"I know… but I don't have the money."

"Exactly why people call you poor," Cassius laughed.

The two chuckled, but Regina's glare snapped them back to attention. They resumed their work in silence, the room filled only with the clicks of switches and hums of the plant.

✳✳✳

Suddenly, an alarm blared through the command center.

"What's that?" Cassius barked, twisting in his chair.

Regina leaned over the main panel, eyes scanning the readouts. "There's a fire in the right wing!" she shouted. "Barnaby! Callum! Deploy the robots—now!"

"Working on it!" Callum snapped. He shoved his chair back, fist slamming down on the red deployment button.

Barnaby, pale-faced, rushed to the phone and punched in the code. "Smog brigade, initiate protocol S4!" he barked into the receiver.

The room exploded into motion. Chairs scraped the floor as workers scattered across the control center, fingers flying over buttons and switches. Every move felt frantic, every second slipping away. Cassius and Callum rolled to separate panels, yanking levers to reroute power and trigger containment protocols.

Above them, the large red glass tube—the Master Alarm—sat dark and silent… for now. Its looming presence cast a shadow, a final warning no one dared to think about.

Five more alarms screamed through the room.

"What the hell is going on? There are too many alarms!" the man at the desk shouted, his voice rising with panic. He grabbed the nearest telephone, hands trembling.

Cassius spun his chair toward the main console, seized the emergency line, and dialed. "All hands on deck! This is a code-red emergency! Repeat, code red—all hands on deck!"

Sweat streamed down their faces as they scrambled through emergency protocols. Levers were pulled to redirect power flow. Buttons slammed down to activate cooling systems. Switches flipped wildly to deploy backup generators. Each frantic motion bought them seconds—but it wasn't enough. Alarms layered over each other until the sound became unbearable. Systems overloaded faster than they could respond, blinking red warnings flashing across every screen.

Then, without warning, the Master Alarm glowed. The red glass tube pulsed with light, releasing a low, vibrating hum that filled the room and made the floor tremble beneath their boots.

Callum froze for a split second—then lunged for the phone. "Mayday, mayday, mayday!" he screamed. "Plant NC71 is going down! We need help—fast!"

"Sir!" a voice cried out, "The robots are down. There are none left!"

"What?" Callum choked.

"Yes! Cameras show sabotage—a surge overloaded their systems. They're fried!"

Cassius gripped the phone, his face pale. "Initiate protocol E17. Abandon base. Now!"

The building shuddered as the first explosion hit. Sparks rained from the ceiling.

"Brace for impact!"

Two more deafening blasts rocked the command center—and then everything vanished into smoke and fire.

Eric sat in his home office, surrounded by sleek hologram walls pulsing faintly with soft blue light. Only one remained clear—a window framing the vast cityscape. From here, he could see it all: the towering skyscrapers, the endless skyways, the city his work helped power.

He wasn't alone. Four holograms of NASA scientists hovered around his desk—real people, but physical presence was unnecessary these days.

"I hear your company is about to release a new chip, Mr. Johansen," one of the engineers began.

"Yes," Eric replied. "We managed to fast-track a prototype for testing. There are still some irregularities, but we're focused on fixing them. You're one of our testers, so I wanted your feedback."

"The chip is working better than I imagined," said Dr. Morales, adjusting his virtual glasses. "Our tests show it improves aeronautical control. Combined with that new processor board you released a few weeks ago, our ship's performance exceeded expectations."

"At Nanocom, we're committed to our customers," Eric responded smoothly.

Dr. Patel, the lead engineer, nodded. "Let's talk about our new rocket. Its propulsion systems are stronger than anything we've built before. With a few more adjustments, we think it could break out of the solar system."

Eric blinked. "What is this about?"

Dr. Liao leaned forward. "Mr. Johansen, we'd like Nanocom to manufacture parts no one else can. Your team delivered that chip in record time. And because Nanocom specializes in nanotechnology, we want you involved in spacecraft systems—chips, circuit boards—everything."

Eric sat back, considering. "I'm honored. I'd gladly accept, but that's above my pay grade. I'll have to run it by Jamal Rao."

Dr. Patel smiled. "We already spoke to him. He approved the project."

Eric's eyebrows rose. "Perfect. Still, we'll need to pitch it to the board. Have NASA send an ambassador—Jamal and I will present the deal, and your team can handle the technical details. Honestly, it's a great plan."

"Thank you for your time, Mr. Johansen," Dr. Patel added. "We'll contact you after the board meeting. I'll personally make sure the ambassador is there."

"Thank you for trusting us."

"It's our pleasure."

The four engineers vanished, their holograms blinking out.

Eric exhaled and said, "Bank, call Jamal Rao. Normal frequency."

"Yes, sir."

A hologram of Jamal materialized a moment later.

"Hey, Eric. What's up?" Jamal greeted casually.

"I just finished with NASA. This partnership could be huge for us," Eric said. "They're serious about expanding space travel—and President Costello's backing it."

"I know. It's a good opportunity," Jamal agreed.

"Then what's the holdup? Matt told me the AN19 chip issues are minor—some transistor misplacements, nothing major. Honestly, I thought NASA wanted the chip for janitorial robots. Turns out they're using it on their new Makashi VII rocket. They want us for their aeronautics systems, Jamal. Chips, nanotech—everything."

Jamal sighed. "Yeah… but I'm not sure the board will bite."

"Well, they'd better. This is a rare opportunity."

"I know," Jamal admitted. "Look, I need you to come in. We'll talk this through—and there's another problem. Some of our older robot models might've been hacked. We've had accidents in a few factories. I need you to check their firewalls and security measures—see if we scrap them or not."

Eric stiffened. "On the weekend?"

"I know. But it's urgent. Not many people will be around—just wear normal clothes."

There was a pause before Eric let out a long sigh. "Okay. I'll be there."

The hologram vanished, leaving Eric alone with the sprawling city beyond his window.

"Bank, book a car and get Amy on the line. I'll change quickly."

"As you wish, sir."

Eric hurried to his closet, swapping his suit for a white t-shirt and jeans. Grabbing his communicator, he moved briskly down the stairs to the front door. White sports shoes appeared on the porch, and robotic arms laced them tightly. Without pausing, Eric stepped onto the waiting hoverboard, letting it glide him to the curb where the car stood ready. He slid inside, dropped his communicator into the cup holder, and clipped his earpiece in place. The car shot forward—faster than expected. Eric gripped the seat, his earpiece nearly slipping free.

Outside, the city flashed past in a silver blur—the gleaming towers, neon-lit skyways, and endless streams of hovercars weaving through the air. On any other day, Eric might have admired the view. But not today. Not with NASA's proposal hanging over his head… and a potential security breach waiting at the office.

Eric exhaled slowly, steadying his nerves. *I have to be ready for Jamal.*

The car entered a tunnel, its lights illuminating the smooth, curved walls as they sped through. But Eric's mind was already racing ahead—planning, calculating, anticipating the meeting to come. Suddenly, the car jolted to a stop. Eric lurched forward, saved only by the seatbelt as his chest slammed back against the seat.

"What the hell?" he gasped, heart hammering.

The tunnel was pitch black. The car's headlights were dead, and the tunnel's lights had gone out completely. Shapes of other vehicles sat motionless ahead, barely visible as Eric's eyes adjusted.

"What just happened?"

Instinctively, Eric waited for Bank's voice. Silence.

"Bank? Bank?"

No response.

"Bank, answer me!"

Nothing.

Weird... A chill ran down Eric's spine. *What's wrong with Bank?*

"Amy?" he called, his voice tense. "Amy, what's going on? Talk to me."

His earpiece stayed silent—no voice, no static, just dead air.

"What happened to my AI systems?"

The ground trembled beneath him. Somewhere behind, a crash echoed through the tunnel.

Eric's breath caught. "Oh my god…"

Fumbling for his communicator, Eric tried dialing 911. A message blinked across the screen:

Unable to place connection
Cellular connectivity lost
Error 101

"Bank? Amy? Anybody—respond!" Eric shouted, his voice echoing through the silent car.

No one answered.

Another distant boom thundered through the tunnel. Eric's chest tightened as panic clawed at him. *How am I supposed to get out of here?*

The ground quaked beneath him. Eric gripped the seat, pressing back as hard as he could, grateful—just barely—for the car's shell protecting him.

And then… he waited.

And waited.

And waited.

And waited.

The shaking finally stopped.

For one brief, fragile moment, Eric thought it was over. Relief almost hit him—until he realized the darkness hadn't lifted. The air felt heavier.

A wave of dizziness hit him as the tunnel trembled again. By the time he steadied himself, Eric realized how hot it had become—trapped, suffocating heat pressing in from every side. He'd been sitting too long. He had to move.

Stretching his arms over the seat, he leaned forward—too fast. His watch clipped the side window with a sharp crack.

Eric froze, staring at the jagged line now cutting through the glass. His mouth dropped open. *What...?* The watch was well-made, sure. But strong enough to crack reinforced car glass?

Heart racing, Eric slammed his fist into the window. Another fracture shot across it.

Again.

And again.

Finally, the window shattered—glass shards exploding into the tunnel.

Eric unclipped his seatbelt and crawled through the jagged frame. As he tumbled out, he hit the asphalt hard, his legs weak and trembling from sitting too long. For a moment, he stayed there, gasping for air, the heat pressing down on him from all sides. But he was free. Collapsing against the pavement, Eric sucked in the hot, stale air—grateful, if only for a second, to still be alive.

Slowly, he forced himself upright, blinking against the darkness. All around him, cars sat frozen in place, scattered like debris. Through the eerie silence, he could hear the faint sounds of people calling out from inside—trapped, confused, and scared. Eric clenched his jaw, the weight of it all settling heavily on his shoulders. He knew exactly what he had to do.

He had to get everyone out.

He had to evacuate the tunnel.

CHAPTER

06

There were no sirens. No distant hum of engines. Eric had expected the debris to be cleared quickly—robots swarming in to save them—but nothing happened. Minutes stretched into an hour. Groups of people huddled together in the dark, whispering to ease their panic.

Some had managed to break free from their cars, and Eric helped at least five others crawl out of shattered windows or jammed doors. But visibility was awful—he could barely see three feet ahead. Beyond that, the tunnel swallowed everything in blackness. He had no idea how many others were still trapped deeper inside.

Only ten people gathered near him now, all of them confused, shivering, and trying to understand what had just happened. Somewhere close, Eric heard a mother murmuring soft words to quiet her crying baby while the group argued about what to do.

"We should punch our way out like we did for the others," someone suggested.

"Are you crazy?" another snapped. "Glass is one thing, but we're boxed in now. We got lucky before—that's not gonna work here."

"Whatever you're thinking, hurry it up," grumbled a man farther back. "We're still in a tunnel."

"Excuse me, but maybe we should actually figure out how to get out of this mess," a woman's voice shot back.

"Yeah, right," a father muttered bitterly. "Talking's not feeding my kid. He's starving."

"Okay, quit your whining," someone else barked.

"Hey! I'm just saying—time's ticking."

"Yeah, we get it," the woman growled. "That's not helping."

"Fine, then what's your plan?"

There was a long pause before a voice spoke from the back, "We can go forward or backward. Those are our choices."

Another voice chimed in, "I vote backward. That's where we came in—maybe the entrance is clear enough by now."

"Backward?" someone shot back. "The entrance is blocked, remember? Debris everywhere. We'll waste time, or worse—get trapped. I say forward. There might be more people. Maybe someone found a way out."

"But that way's darker."

"Doesn't matter," someone else said. "There's nothing for us back there. Forward's our only shot."

"They could've already escaped ahead of us."

"I can still hear voices," a woman whispered.

"Going backward means retracing our steps. We'll get more clues."

"I don't care about clues," the father growled. "I care about getting my son out."

"That's how we get out."

The bickering built, rising louder and more frantic—until Eric finally snapped.

"Enough!" His voice cut through the dark like a blade.

Everyone froze, turning toward him.

"Look, I get it," Eric said, his voice steady but low. "I'm stuck here too. My car's dead. My AI systems—gone. My communicator doesn't work. You're all dealing with the same thing. But arguing like this? It's not helping. Standing here debating while your kid's hungry—it won't get us out."

A heavy silence settled. No one interrupted.

Eric took a breath and pushed forward. "It doesn't matter which way we go, forward or backward. We move. We examine everything as we go. Somewhere, there's a way out—we just haven't found it yet. We'll hit setbacks, yeah. But we will escape."

There was a pause, then a muttered voice from the shadows, bitter but resigned, "Yeah… easy for you to say."

Eric ignored it. He wasn't done yet.

"Let's start walking."

The group fell in line, their footsteps echoing through the tunnel as they moved toward the entrance. Eric kept one hand against the wall, guiding himself forward through the darkness, but there was nothing—no side exits, no breaks, no hint of rescue—just endless concrete swallowing the sound of their breathing.

They trudged in silence until someone muttered bitterly, "Well, looks like we're screwed again. I've been searching like a madman—there's nothing. No way out."

Eric's patience snapped. "Fine. If you want to sit here and die, that's your decision."

Without waiting for a response, he pushed forward, leaving them behind in their doubt. His fingers skimmed along the rough wall until suddenly he felt it—something cold and solid. Metal. He froze. Heart pounding, Eric leaned in. It was a doorknob—fixed right into the tunnel wall.

"Guys!" he called out, voice echoing off the concrete. "I found something—a door."

The others scrambled over, disbelief etched across their faces as they gathered around him.

"Why the hell is there a door down here?" one man asked, suspicion tightening his voice.

Eric shook his head. "I think I know. But let's get through it first. I'll explain later."

Gripping the knob, Eric twisted hard. It didn't move.

"Locked," he muttered under his breath. "Of course."

"Move over," another voice snapped. A man in a dark coat shoved past him and dug something from his pocket. Without hesitation, he knelt and worked the lock with practiced hands.

Seconds later, the lock gave way with a heavy click. The door creaked open, revealing a narrow stairwell winding upward, the walls damp and crumbling.

"Well... looks like we're climbing," Eric said, swallowing hard. He stepped inside first and started up the steps without waiting for a vote. The others followed, their footsteps heavy against the metal stairs. The climb was brutal—twisting, steep, endless. Every few steps, the rusted metal groaned beneath their weight.

"Can we stop?" someone panted behind him. "Please... just a minute."

Eric paused, resting his hands against the damp wall but not turning back. "Okay. Just a few minutes. We don't have water, and we don't know how long this goes."

"We should've stayed," another muttered. "This is insane."

Eric closed his eyes, breathing slowly and steadily. "We're too far in. Keep moving."

After a brief rest and a few fresh arguments, the group pushed on. The air grew colder the higher they climbed, and the only sounds were their ragged breathing and the dull clank of boots against metal. No one spoke anymore. There was nothing left to say.

Eric refused to stop. The only way out was up.

At last, they reached the top. A door waited, pale light seeping through the edges. Eric pushed it open and blinked against the sudden change. Before them stretched a dense forest—towering trees, sunlight filtering down through the leaves, and the sharp scent of earth and greenery. It hit him all at once, a shocking contrast to the suffocating darkness below. Eric stood there, stunned. How deep had that tunnel run? They had surfaced in the middle of nowhere.

He turned toward the others. "It's getting dark. I suggest everyone find a place inside to sleep. I'll stay out here for now—just to keep watch."

Someone scoffed behind him. "Forget it. I'm walking home."

Eric spun toward the voice. "If you walk now, you'll wander straight into a powerless city. The lights are off. The doors won't open. You'll get lost out there. Stay. Rest. We'll figure it out in the morning."

"Why can't we just call 911?" someone asked, exhaustion sharpening their words.

"Believe me," Eric said, his voice flat. "I tried in the tunnel. No signal. Nothing."

"Same here," another muttered from near the treeline. "Towers must be down."

The words hung heavy in the air. One by one, the group gave in—silent now, heads down—as they shuffled past Eric and toward the old house nearby.

Eric lingered by the door, watching until the last person disappeared inside. Only then did he pull it closed behind him, the latch clicking softly. He leaned back against the wall, feeling the weight of the day settle deep in his chest.

For a moment, there was only silence.

Then, from somewhere deeper in the house, a single light flickered to life.

CHAPTER

07

E ric opened his eyes and stared up at the canopy of trees overhead. For a moment, his mind was blank—unsure where he was or how he had gotten there. The forest looked almost too perfect—too green, too still. A familiar suspicion crept in.

No way this is real.

"Bank, are you tricking me again?" he muttered.

Silence.

"Bank?"

Still no response.

Eric sat up slowly, scanning his surroundings. The forest was beautiful, but he wasn't so easily fooled. He figured he must've sleepwalked into his living room, and Bank was just running the forest theme again— probably looping it for effect.

He reached down and pressed his hand to the ground. It felt soft— almost like the fur of a kitten. But when he lifted his palm, a brownish substance clung to it. Dirt.

That's... new.

Eric stood and took a cautious step forward toward the nearest tree. He fully expected to touch the cold, hard wall of his apartment—because that's how it always worked. Still, he had to try.

Five steps.

Four.

Three.

Two.

One.

All he had to do now was reach.

Reach for the tree—or the glass.

His hand met rough bark. Real bark. Jagged and uneven beneath his fingertips. For a moment, a wild sense of joy flared inside him, pulling his eyebrows up and spreading a grin across his face.

It's real...

But the happiness faded just as quickly. Something felt off. Why hadn't the scene shifted? Why hadn't Bank said anything? Panic flickered through him.

What if I overslept? What if I'm late for work? The thoughts pulsed through Eric's tired brain, each one landing harder than the last.

Then, like a dam breaking, the memories of the last twenty-four hours came rushing back. His eyes widened. He stumbled back from the tree and broke into a run, crashing through the underbrush. He didn't care where—he just needed to find the city, any sign of civilization.

Please... let this be another simulation. Let me wake up.

Eric crested a hill and scanned the horizon, heart hammering in his chest. He searched everywhere, desperate for any sign—buildings, roads, people. There had to be something. He couldn't have just wandered out here on his own. But all he could see were endless stretches of forest, rolling hills, and open prairies. No roads. No city. Nothing.

Chest tightening, Eric turned and began the long trudge back to the house—the one he and a group of strangers had stayed in the night before. It was the only landmark he had. When he reached it, Eric opened the door and stepped inside—for the first time, really looking at it. The house was old but beautiful in a way he hadn't noticed before. The living room was lined with three worn couches, and an old LED screen hung mounted on the wall. Below it sat a boxy device with physical buttons—something ancient, designed to control the screen.

His gaze shifted to a symbol hanging on the left wall. Curious, Eric stepped closer. It was a painting—or maybe a print—of a man holding a knife, one foot planted firmly on the chest of a fallen robot.

The image stirred something deep in his memory. Suddenly, he was back in eighth grade—sitting at his desk, taking notes on his computer while his teacher moved to the front of the room. A holoboard glowed behind her as she spoke.

"Vanessa, did you forget to turn in your homework again?" the teacher asked, voice sharp but tired.

"Yes, Mrs. Stuart," a girl mumbled from the back. "I'll turn it in today."

"Make sure you turn it in for half credit. Now, class, today we're going to learn about the Anti-Tech Revolution of 2060. Shandra, bring it up."

The holoboard flickered, then displayed a symbol: a man stomping on a robot. The teacher gestured toward it. "This was the symbol used by a group called the Superiors. With technology taking over the country, this group staged riots—blowing up factories, shops, and even houses—all to destroy the robots. They were determined to reclaim control. One of their safe houses is thought to be hidden somewhere in the mountains."

The memory faded as a chill ran down Eric's spine. He stared at the same symbol now hanging on the living room wall.

That's where I am, he realized. *I'm in one of their safe houses... right here in the city. The center of operations for the anarchy my grandparents warned me about. The Superiors.*

Footsteps creaked on the stairs. A child's voice called out, "Mommy, when are we going back home?"

A softer voice answered, "Just relax, son. We'll be home soon enough."

Another voice chimed in, uneasy. "How long are we gonna be here?"

Someone else mumbled, "A few months... maybe even years. I don't exactly know myself."

Then a man in his early thirties came down the stairs, glancing around the room. "How was the night watch?" he asked.

"Pretty good," Eric replied. "No one attacked us."

"Yeah..."

The man's words trailed off as he froze mid-step. Eric followed his gaze and realized he was staring at the symbol on the wall.

"I think this place was a safe house for the Superiors," Eric said quietly. "They probably planned their attacks right here." He glanced back at the man. "But don't worry. The Superiors were wiped out a long time ago. The group's extinct now."

The man nodded slowly. "Thanks for telling me... I was scared."

"Why were you scared?" Eric asked.

"I don't know... I mean, I heard stories. A relative of mine was killed by them. They were a pretty hot topic back in school. My dad even ran into a few of them once."

Eric nodded. The man came over and sat beside him on the couch. They both stared at the floor for a while, saying nothing.

"Well," Eric finally sighed. "Looks like we're stuck here."

"You never know," the man offered. "The power could come back on soon."

"We'll see what happens. What's your name?"

"John," the man said. "John Verricker. You?"

"Eric Johansen."

"Oh."

They sat in silence again, the weight of the moment settling between them.

After a beat, Eric spoke. "I went out this morning to look for the tunnel... but it's gone. Or maybe it's buried. Either way, I couldn't find it. I don't think it's a good idea to head out blindly right now. We have no idea where we are, and there's nothing but forest for miles. If we're stuck here a few days, we should at least figure out if this place is livable."

John shrugged. "Be my guest."

Eric ambled through the house, pausing as he entered the dining room. A large table sat in the center, surrounded by ten chairs. Various paintings were scattered across the white walls, their colors faded with time.

What amazed Eric most was the room on the left.

A beautiful sink—larger than any he'd seen before—sat beneath a window that overlooked the yard. Against one wall stood an ancient stovetop, its surface scratched and worn with age. Drawers and cabinets lined the room, their handles dulled from years of use. In the corner, two silver doors stood stacked one on top of the other, each with controls he didn't recognize.

Eric had never seen such a place. He couldn't imagine why there were so many tiny doors in one section of a house. Curiosity getting the better of him, he opened one of the cabinets—and gasped.

Blades.

They covered every inch of the space from top to bottom. Eric reached for one, carefully lifting the handle. Unlike the dull utensils he was used to, this knife was sharpened to a deadly point. He turned it over in his hands, wondering what it had been used for. As far as he knew, the Superiors didn't rely on knives as weapons.

He heard footsteps coming from the stairs, but he continued his exploration. Eric opened another door and was hit with a foul stench. His nose wrinkled as he stepped inside a dark gray room. Open shelves lined the walls, filled with tools of all shapes and sizes. In the corner, something unusual caught his eye—an old bicycle with only one wheel and a light bulb mounted on top. Its black paint was chipped, the silver rods slightly bent, but the pedals remained intact.

He hesitated, then placed his foot on the pedal and pushed.

The bulb flickered to life.

Startled, Eric pulled his foot back. The light vanished.

Heart pounding, he tried again. The harder he pedaled, the brighter the light glowed. Eric stared, mesmerized. He had never seen a light function this way. Back home, everything was controlled by Bank or Amy. There had never been a reason to question how things worked.

A sharp pang of hunger pulled him from his thoughts. He hadn't eaten since the previous afternoon. The realization hit him hard—how were they supposed to find food out here?

He made his way back to the living room, where the rest of the group was gathered.

For the first time, Eric took in the twelve unfamiliar faces. Two families sat together, each with at least two kids. Two women whispered quietly to one another while another man sat beside John. Before they did anything else, Eric knew they had to recognize the situation for what it was and prepare for what was to come.

Shuffling his feet, he cleared his throat. "Um, hello, I guess."

No one responded.

Eric frowned. "Why are you guys staring at me?"

One of the fathers, his arm wrapped protectively around his son, gave him a sharp look. "Because you're the one who got us here. Whatever you plan to do next, you should share with us."

Eric swallowed. His mouth felt dry. "Okay then. I need you to listen carefully." He took a steadying breath. "We just escaped from the tunnel, which was a bad experience for all of us. Now we're stuck in this old house, and none of us knows how long we'll be here."

He glanced around the room. "We will survive, that's for sure. We just need to find food and supplies. There are trees outside that might bear fruit. We can also forage for vegetables."

Contrary to what Eric had hoped, no one seemed uplifted by his words. Frightened whispers spread across the room, a few grumbles mixed in. Some of the group stood and wandered off, eager to explore the house for themselves.

Eric felt awkward. He hadn't expected a rousing speech, but the lack of reaction still stung. Quietly, he retreated to the couch, buried his face in his hands, and exhaled.

CHAPTER

08

E ric plucked apples with John and one of the fathers from the group in the fading afternoon light.

John had continued exploring the house earlier and stumbled upon a massive garden tucked away behind the backyard. The garden overflowed with plants and trees, their leaves heavy with fruit and vegetables. The air was thick with the scent of lavender and rosemary, the rich aroma almost dizzying in the warm breeze.

After the disastrous meeting in the living room, Eric—once he recovered from his embarrassment—showed everyone the light he had discovered. They were equally amazed and stunned that electricity could work without an AI system to control it.

Everyone was even more astonished by the room filled with white drawers and cabinets. Eric showed them the knives he'd found, and one of the older women explained they were used for cutting fruit and vegetables.

The group searched through the drawers, pulling out spoons, forks, knives, and cups. There were even metal pots and pans—actual cooking tools to prepare food by hand. Eric was ecstatic at the discovery. The idea of preparing food manually thrilled him. He had never heard of such an unbelievable thing. Some of the items they found were unfamiliar to everyone. Eric pulled out a wooden handle with a flat piece of metal attached, an enormous pair of tweezers, and a large spoon with a deep, cup-shaped bowl. None of it made much sense.

Eric realized that in all his years focused on work, he had never given much thought to how people lived in the past. History class had only offered scattered pieces—stories of wars, global conflicts, prosperous eras, and dark ages. No one had ever talked about utensils.

He placed the apples carefully into an old basket he found in the food-making room. As he worked, the sound of birds chirping nearby made him pause. He glanced around, startled. He'd never heard birds in real life—not like this. Back home, birds only existed in the AI themes—background noise generated for effect. Eric couldn't see them, but their songs filled the air. Suddenly, a piece of fruit dropped to the ground beside him, and from the shadows, a bird emerged. Its feathers were a vibrant blue, with a patch of white on its belly.

Eric's mind drifted back to the day he visited the park. There had been a fountain, and the speakers played a birdsong theme that seemed so real at the time. But this—this was different. Even staring straight at the bird, he struggled to believe it wasn't some projection or hologram.

After gathering all the apples within reach, Eric moved on to the cucumbers. He plucked them from the vines, carefully nestling them into the basket. A man who looked to be in his mid-thirties worked beside him, silent at first.

Finally, the man spoke. "The sun's pretty intense. I wonder if the people who lived here ever overheated."

Eric smirked. "Yeah, this would be the perfect graveyard for the Superiors. Still, how did they survive in this heat?"

The man shrugged. "Not sure."

A heaviness settled over Eric as he wiped the sweat from his brow. "How long are we going to be here? How are we supposed to survive until the power is restored?"

The man let out a slow breath. "It's hard to tell, but I'm sure in a few months, the power will return. I'm just speculating, though. I don't really know."

"Does anyone know?" Eric asked.

"Probably not," the man admitted.

Both men continued harvesting cucumbers from the vines, their movements slow and methodical beneath the weight of the afternoon sun. Seeing that his basket was nearly full, Eric asked, "What is your name?"

"Arthur Chalmers."

"Eric Johansen."

"Nice to meet you, Eric."

"You too, Arthur. I'm going to pluck a few oranges before I head inside."

"You do that. I'll see you later."

Eric wandered toward the orange trees, the basket heavy in his arms. Yet, as he neared the grove, a strange happiness swelled in his chest—a deep, almost childlike bliss he hadn't felt since... well, since before any of this. The feeling was overwhelming. No theme, no simulation, had ever stirred this kind of joy. The garden, the sunlight, the rich, earthy smell of growing things—it all felt too real, too perfect. Eric fought the sudden urge to hop, skip, and spin like a child let loose in a playground.

But the ground was uneven, and Eric lost his footing. He stumbled forward, the basket slipping from his grip. Fruit scattered across the grass. As Eric steadied himself, something half-buried in the dirt caught his eye. He crouched down and pulled it free—an old book, its cover faded but intact. It was lighter than his tablet, almost fragile in his hands.

Curious, Eric examined the cover more closely. The title, which was faint but still legible, read "The Cat in the Hat." A picture of a tall, grinning cat wearing a red and white striped hat and a red bowtie stared back at him.

Eric blinked in disbelief. As far as he knew, books like this only existed on tablets. Physical copies were just... stories—artifacts of the past. Almost instinctively, he swiped his finger across the cover, expecting the page to turn. Nothing happened.

He tried again—still nothing.

Confused, Eric swiped harder and faster until frustration got the better of him, and he flung the book to the ground.

That's when it happened.

The book flipped open as it landed, pages fanning out in the dirt.

Startled, Eric grabbed it and stared.

The paper was soft and delicate, creased from age. He ran his fingers along the edge of the page, feeling the texture—thin, almost brittle, yet somehow still intact. A memory surfaced—an old conversation with Bank about books made of paper and glue. He'd wondered what it would feel like to hold one, to flip real pages instead of tapping a screen. He'd read hundreds of stories but never like this.

Eric sat down beneath a tree, cradling the book in his hands. Slowly, carefully, he turned the page. As he read, his mind drifted back—back to first grade, to his old classroom during silent reading time. He could see himself sitting at his desk, a tablet propped in front of him. On the screen, the cover of *The Cat in the Hat* stared back, just like this.

Snapping out of the memory, Eric stared at the book in awe. *It's the same story. The exact same book I read as a kid.* He flipped through more pages, marveling at the colorful illustrations—hand-drawn pictures printed right there on the paper.

"There you are!"

Startled, Eric looked up and saw John standing a few feet away, hands on his hips.

"Where were you? Everyone's eating dinner."

"Oh... I was just... reading a book."

John blinked. "A book? Are you out of your mind? How can you read a book after the blackout?"

"I'll explain everything. Gosh... I forgot to get oranges."

John smirked. "We've got plenty. Let's eat."

Eric gave the book one last glance, then grabbed his basket and walked with John back to the house, the weight of the discovery still heavy in his hands.

CHAPTER

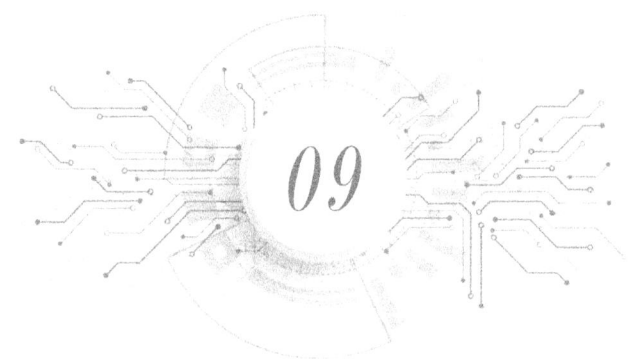

A s a new day began, Eric wandered through the house, munching an apple.

So many discoveries, he thought. *The food-making items, the light, the book—what else might they uncover?*

His mind drifted back to the night before when he'd stumbled upon an office tucked away at the end of the hall. Inside, he'd found an old wooden desk, a comfortable chair, and dozens of framed pictures—bugs, spiders, beetles, and insects covering nearly every inch of wall space.

But what truly caught Eric's attention were the shelves—rows and rows of books, more than he'd ever seen in one place. He scanned the titles in disbelief, realizing he didn't even recognize most of them.

Windows 98: How to Operate the Software, The Hobbit, Great Expectations—the names meant little to him, but the sight of them left him so stunned he nearly dropped his apple.

Still curious, Eric wandered into the gray room—the one with the bicycle rigged to the strange light. Shelves lined the walls, cluttered with items that looked like relics from another world. He examined them one by one: minuscule sabers topped with crosses, tightly coiled metal spirals capped at both ends, slender bars with crescent-shaped heads. Tools or weapons—he couldn't tell. Eric stared, unable to even guess how these objects worked or what they were meant to do.

Eventually, Eric returned to the living room and sank into a chair, finishing his apple. Arthur was already coming down the stairs. He plopped down across from Eric with a sigh.

"How do you think people even survived back then?" Arthur asked, shaking his head. "Without even an AI system! I swear, it's only been two days, and I keep expecting Arnold to show up with my breakfast and bring the car around."

"Tell me about it," Eric replied. "I found some weird thing that turned out to be an old copy of *The Cat in the Hat.* I heard books were made of something called paper back then. But honestly, I couldn't even figure out how to open it at first."

"And that room with those knives and stuff? I didn't even know that's what it was for."

"Yeah, me neither. I just knew some of it because... well, I'm a bit of a history buff."

Arthur grinned. "Dang, that's a nice rhyme."

Eric smirked. "Yeah, speaking of rhymes, they were pretty popular back in ancient times. They used to turn them into something called poetry. People loved the way words were put together to... I don't know... stir emotions or whatever."

"Okay, well, when you put it that way, it sounds boring," Arthur sniggered.

"Hey, that hurt," Eric shot back in a mock wounded voice.

They both laughed—genuine, lighthearted—for the first time in days. The sound echoed through the old house like a small piece of normalcy.

After a moment, Eric sobered and leaned forward. "You know... I think we should organize a team to search for supplies."

Arthur blinked. "Supplies from where?"

"The city," Eric said simply.

Arthur's eyes widened. "What do you mean? You're not... you're not going to steal them, are you?"

"That's exactly what I plan to do," Eric answered without hesitation.

Arthur sat back, stunned. "Eric, are you sure that's a good idea? I mean... what if the power comes back on? You'll be breaking the law."

"There are no laws in a blackout, Arthur. I don't like it either, but it's survival." Eric paused, glancing toward the staircase. "Until everyone's awake for the morning pep talk—"

"One of us is," a voice interrupted.

Both men turned to see John walking down the stairs. He joined them at the table, his expression grim but focused.

"Arthur, hear me out," John said. "We've only been here two days, but supplies are already dwindling. We need to head into the city... see if there are other survivors. Maybe there's something—someone—left."

Arthur hesitated. "Just one question... Based on what we know, the blackout is citywide. So... shouldn't we be looking for a way out of here? We could try to reach a neighboring city or town, start fresh... live our lives there."

"You know," John started slowly, "that might not be a bad idea, Arthur—"

Eric cut him off. "There's nowhere to go. I doubt any of us knows the way out of this place. None of us even has a map. Leaving the house just means wandering through miles of forest... with no car and no service. It's a death sentence. The best thing we can do is stay here... adjust... survive. There's no one to call for help."

Arthur let out a long breath. "All right," he finally said.

The three sat in silence until Eric finally stood and beckoned the others to follow. They wandered outside for a walk through the garden, their steps slow as they took in the scattered patches of green still thriving around them. Fruit trees and vegetable plants sprouted here and there, surprising in their abundance.

Eric couldn't contain his quiet excitement as he moved through the rows, realizing how strange it felt to be bonding with two men he'd only met because of such unfortunate, bizarre circumstances. For a moment, as they passed a cabbage plant, Eric forced himself to look away, trying not to dwell on the conversation drifting toward the Superiors.

Hours later, after breakfast, Eric called everyone to the living room for his usual daily speech.

John and Arthur stood at his side as Eric faced the group. "As you all know, our supplies are dwindling," he began. "John, Arthur, and I have come up with a plan. We're going into the city to bring back what we need. We'll use the light I showed you—powered by the bicycle. If we generate enough power, we should be able to light our way through the tunnel."

He paused, scanning the group. "We'll need two people pedaling the bike while the others help guide and steady it. It's too heavy to ride, so the pedaling's just for the light. We'll have to work together to keep it moving."

"How will you get to the city?" someone asked.

"Through the tunnel, of course."

A groan rose from the back. "Gosh, I don't want to climb all those steps again."

"Isn't the tunnel blocked?" another voice called. "How are you even going to get through?"

"Maybe other survivors moved the debris," Eric replied. "We might be able to squeeze our way in."

The group murmured among themselves until, finally, two women stepped forward. The parents drifted outside, letting their children play, while the volunteers joined Eric, John, and Arthur.

One was tall, with creamy skin and a flame-red bob. "I'm Sabrina," she said.

The other, with golden skin and jet-black hair, gave a simple nod. "Sarah."

The five of them filed into the room with the old bicycle and gathered around it. Eric explained how it worked and showed them the light rigged to the frame.

"John and Arthur will pedal to power the light," Eric continued. "Sabrina and Sarah—help steady the back and spin the tire by hand if you need to. I'll lead, carrying the front."

They practiced twice, testing their coordination until Eric was satisfied they could manage it. Then, grabbing old bags they found in the office and looping them over their shoulders, the group made their way to the tunnel entrance. Without a word, they pushed open the heavy door and stepped into the darkness. John and Arthur manned the pedals while Eric took point, leading the way as the beam of light flickered across the narrow path ahead.

Eric gasped when the full descent came into view—an endless stretch of stairs spiraling down. They moved carefully, the steepness making every step a test of balance, especially with the weight of the bike.

It wasn't long before Sabrina's breath hitched. "Can we stop?" she asked, her voice trembling.

Eric immediately agreed. They set the bike down, pausing to catch their breath. After a few minutes, they resumed, forcing themselves onward.

When they finally reached the bottom, Eric froze, heart hammering. Bodies—dozens of them—were sprawled across the ground. He couldn't tell whether to panic or feel relief. It was like walking into a horror movie. There was no blood, no sign of violence. Just still, lifeless bodies. Many looked young. Some were even children. Eric stood there, numb, the grim truth sinking in. They must have been trapped when the blackout hit… no way out, no airflow. They suffocated.

Sunlight bled through a small opening at the tunnel's far end. It seemed other survivors had clawed their way through the debris and escaped.

Seeing the light, Eric made a quick decision. "Leave the bike here," he said. The weight lifted—literally—as they lowered it to the ground.

Eric pulled out the thread. One by one, they tied it around their fingers, anchoring it to the tunnel walls before stepping out into the city. The scene that met them was worse than anything Eric could have imagined. Cars clogged the streets in every direction. Passengers still sat inside, their eyes closed, heads slumped. For a moment, they almost looked like they were sleeping. But Eric knew better. They were dead.

The group split up, spreading through the maze of abandoned vehicles. Eric gripped his thread tightly, refusing to let go. Without it, there was no way back. He passed countless cars. Some had shattered windows, hinting at desperate escape attempts. Most remained untouched—silent tombs. Eric pressed forward, moving deeper into the city. The sidewalks were littered with hoverboard riders, their bodies twisted where they'd fallen. Piles of corpses lay outside buildings, stacked like trash alongside robots—lifeless, stiff, their eyes dull.

Eric's throat tightened. This wasn't a city anymore. It was a graveyard.

He stopped outside a local warehouse—*Turner Stores, Robot Grab and Go Station*. Carefully, he laid his thread on the sidewalk, marking his path, then kicked the door until it gave way and fell inward with a sharp bang. The place was silent and lifeless, save for a few powered-down robots frozen in place. The only light came from the dusty windows at the front of the store.

Eric moved quickly, scanning the shelves and grabbing whatever seemed useful—spices, baking powder, toilet paper, power bars—and putting them all into his black bag. After raiding the robot courier station, Eric stepped back outside. He stood there for a long moment, staring at the empty street. Just last week, he'd walked this same city, breathing it in, admiring the skyline. Now, he was scavenging to survive.

Nothing of his former world remained—only a handful of strangers lucky enough to still be breathing. He wondered about Jamal, about Matt… or anyone else he knew. A tear welled in his eye and spilled down his cheek. But the answer was everywhere—silent, suffocating.

There was no one left.

Eric looked up at the sky, wondering if they were staring down at him from the heavens. Slowly, he lifted his hand and waved. "Goodbye," he whispered.

There were so many people he wished he could say goodbye to—but this would have to do. His loved ones knew who they were. With a heavy sigh, Eric swung the black bag over his shoulder, picked up the thread, and began the slow walk back to the tunnel. Head down, he retraced every step. When he finally reached the tunnel entrance, he carefully coiled the thread and tucked it into his bag—there was no need for it now. He slipped inside and sat down beside the bike, waiting.

Sabrina arrived next, carrying toiletries and clothing she'd gathered for the group. Not long after, John showed up with groceries. Arthur and Sarah followed, lugging bags filled with medical supplies, hygiene items, and water. With everyone back, they reassembled at the bike. Arthur and John took their places at the pedals, Sabrina and Sarah steadied the back, and Eric lifted the front. The light flickered to life as they retraced their path, moving carefully toward the staircase. When they reached the base, Eric made sure to close the tunnel door behind them—sealing it off so no one could follow.

Halfway up the endless stairs, they stopped for a break, setting the bike on its side. No one spoke. After a few minutes, they started climbing again—slowly but steadily—until, finally, they reached the top.

Their bodies aching, they began the final journey back to the house. As they walked, the forest thick around them, Eric caught a glimmer of red deep in the woods. He slowed, staring. It was a building—small, hidden.

But he said nothing. Kept walking.

When they finally reached the house, everyone drifted toward the food-making room to unload their bags. Eric placed his down, then crossed to John and gripped his shoulder.

John turned, brow furrowed. "What's up?"

"I'm going out for a bit," Eric said.

"What? Eric, you can't go back to the tunnel. We just pulled off the heist."

"No... that's not it. I'm going into the woods. I'll be back in a few minutes."

"Eric, it's—"

"Dangerous. I know." Eric's voice was steady. "But I'll be fine. If I'm not back by nightfall... don't worry."

John exhaled. "Okay."

Without another word, Eric slipped out the front door and followed the path back toward the tunnel. But when he reached the spot where he'd seen the red structure, he veered off, quickening his pace. The building came into view—small, made of wood, weathered by time and the elements.

The door was sealed with an ancient metal latch. Eric tugged and pushed, but the door refused to budge. He considered kicking it down but hesitated. Then, almost by accident, his hand brushed the latch.

Curiosity took over. He jiggled it and felt it shift. He tried again—lifting and twisting—until finally, the latch gave way, and the door creaked open.

The building was barren except for a zipped bag resting on a shelf and a tall wooden box with various knobs on the front. Eric studied the objects carefully. They had to mean something—no one would store them away for years without a reason. He stepped closer, examining the knobs on the tall, brown box. The device was heavy. Between the knobs, he noticed a dial and a small compartment marked with a faint yellow coating. Tucked inside was a small booklet—similar to the one he'd found near the orange trees. Eric took a deep breath. Whatever these things were, they might be important.

He tucked the tall brown box under one arm, slipped the zipped bag into his pocket, and carefully gathered the manual. With everything secured, he turned and started back toward the house.

CHAPTER

10

The old house had begun to feel more like home. Thanks to the fruit they'd gathered and the supplies Eric and the others brought back, their meals slowly improved.

Someone had found an old book in the kitchen, and when Sabrina picked it up, she realized it was a cookbook. Inside were instructions for all kinds of dishes—apple pie among them. Sarah stayed busy organizing the home, so Sabrina recruited John and Arthur to help her try the recipe. They were in the middle of preparing the ingredients when Eric returned from his expedition, carrying two boxes and an old booklet. Without a word, he scurried off to the office to inspect them.

Eric sat down behind the desk and studied the tall box carefully. *What is this curious item?* he wondered. Flipping through the booklet, Eric's eyes widened. It was dated 1934—nearly 200 years ago. It was a miracle it had survived. The booklet called the box a vacuum tube radio. Eric stared, amazed. He had only heard of radios in school—one of humanity's first tools for communication. But he'd never seen one with his own eyes.

If it was really used for communication… and still intact… maybe it could work. Eric's mind raced. *If I could get a signal out, maybe someone's listening. Maybe the White House… or some government agency.*

The house was starting to feel like home, but deep down, Eric knew they couldn't stay forever. At some point, they'd have to return to their lives.

His thoughts drifted to the children. *What kind of future will they have if they're stuck here? If they don't get an education, if they grow up like this… society won't recover. We won't recover.*

Eric's jaw tightened. The radio might be the answer.

He had to try.

Eric twisted the knobs, hoping for a miracle, but nothing happened. He tried again, spinning the dials until, suddenly, the needle shifted—and a short burst of static crackled from the speakers. It lasted barely five seconds, but it was enough. Excitement surged through him. If the radio made that sound, it wasn't dead. His plan could work.

He was about to try again when Sabrina's voice startled him. He'd been so focused that he hadn't heard her enter.

"Dinner's ready, Eric. What do you think you're doing with that box?" she asked, eyeing him.

Eric looked up, blinking. "Oh… I've been looking forward to tonight's meal."

"Uh-huh." She folded her arms. "Now answer the question. What are you doing with that box?"

"Huh?"

"That box of knobs you were messing with just now."

"Oh. The radio. I was testing it—to see if it works."

Sabrina scoffed. "A radio? Radio communication died out long ago."

"Yeah, but… if I can make it work, maybe we'll find someone else out there. Somewhere we can go." He glanced at her. "The blackout destroyed the city. We can't stay here forever."

Sabrina listened, her arms still crossed. When he finished, she shook her head. "Eric, I know you want to help. But fiddling with a box of knobs isn't the answer. Even if it is a radio, what then? How's it going to help us?"

She softened a little. "Come on. I'm sure you're hungry."

Without waiting for a reply, she turned and walked out. Eric hesitated, then followed her to the kitchen. Everyone sat around the table, grinning at the two apple pies—crude and a little overcooked, but they didn't care. After two days of fruit and vegetables, anything different was a treat. Eric took his seat at the head of the table and grabbed a slice. He took a bite, grimacing slightly—it wasn't great—but that didn't matter. It was their first attempt, and it tasted like hope.

After dinner, they lingered at the table, talking. It felt like the beginning of something new. Much like it was for the pilgrims, Eric thought, when Squanto taught them how to grow their own food. Hopefully, their journey wouldn't end in a massacre. Eventually, everyone shuffled off to their rooms for the night.

Eric took a shower with soaps salvaged from the raid that morning. To his surprise, the water still worked—probably gravity-fed from an old rooftop tank—but it was icy cold. He shivered, teeth chattering, wishing he were home. He dressed in nightclothes they'd found—slightly too short for him—and went to his room. It was small, with a narrow bed and a cramped closet. The window overlooked the yard. Then, Eric slipped under the covers and closed his eyes.

But sleep wouldn't come.

His mind raced with everything weighing on him—the impossibility of living in the woods forever. Sure, they could feed themselves for now, but it wouldn't last. Supplies would run out. Others were out there— survivors just like them—and soon, there wouldn't be enough for anyone. Eric's thoughts drifted to his parents. *If only they were here,* he thought bitterly. *They'd know what to do.* But he shoved the memories aside. *There's no time for that. I have to fix this.*

He couldn't let the group down. He'd gotten them this far. He had to find a way to get them home. The radio was the key. It had to be. If it didn't work… they were done. Roadkill. The thought gnawed at him, keeping his eyes wide open in the dark. He wanted to rush back and work on the radio, but there was no light—pitch black.

Frustrated, Eric shot upright in bed, then slid down to the floor. He sat there, head in his hands, forcing himself to think of anything that could keep him awake. Memories came flooding in—disjointed and random. He was a kid riding his tricycle for the first time. He was in college, cramming for finals. He was nervously asking a girl to prom. He was at the gym, pushing through another set of pushups…

And then, just like that, the first rays of sunlight slipped through the window. Without wasting a second, Eric bolted from the room, raced down the stairs, and headed straight for the office. He twisted knobs, flipped switches—desperate—but nothing happened. Not even static. Again and again, he tried. Hours seemed to pass until, just as he was ready to give up, the radio crackled to life.

Eric's heart leapt. It worked.

He nudged the amplifier knob, praying for more than static. The low hum faded, and faint sounds rose from the speakers. It was weak, but it was something. The flickering twig Sarah had lit earlier was already burning low. Eric worked quickly, memorizing the placement of the knobs while he could still see. As the last of the light died, exhaustion caught up with him. There was nothing more he could do now—not in the dark. Eric stumbled upstairs and lay down, finally allowing himself a brief nap.

By the time the sun climbed higher in the sky, Eric was back outside, walking the garden path. He sank beneath a tree, burying his head in his hands.

The radio worked. He heard it.

They had communication.

Why couldn't anyone else see that? If he could reach someone—

anyone—maybe they could trade, rebuild. Maybe they wouldn't have to die out here after all.

But Eric was so swept up in his idea that it never crossed his mind— what if no one else had a working radio? What if no one even heard them?

He didn't care. Not yet. All he could think about was the plan he was hatching for that evening.

CHAPTER

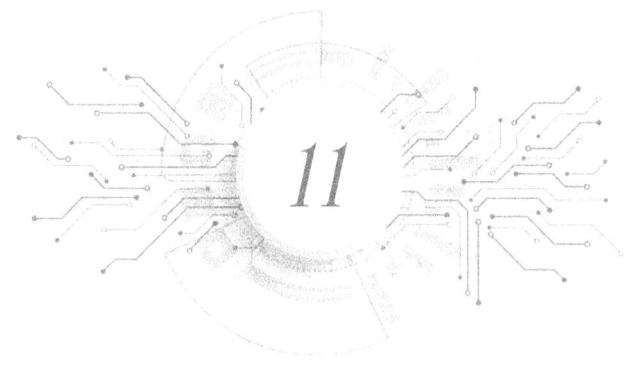

11

S hortly before dinner, Eric noticed the sun was setting. He went into the office, sat down at the desk, and carefully turned the knobs into their memorized positions. Static buzzed, then slowly faded. Eric leaned in, his throat dry, and called out.

"Hello?"

Nothing.

"Hello?"

Still no response. Eric's heart dropped. He had put so much effort into this—hours of work, nights of planning—and he refused to let it fail now.

"Hello?" he tried again, his arms beginning to shake as the silence dragged on.

Footsteps echoed faintly in the hallway, but Eric barely heard them.

"Somebody, please respond. Hello?"

"Eric, why are you talking to yourself like that?" a voice asked.

Eric turned to see John standing in the doorway, a puzzled expression on his face. But he couldn't stop. He turned back toward the radio.

"Come on, please... respond!" His voice cracked, the desperation bleeding through.

He was on the verge of tears. He'd worked so hard—what did it amount to? Nothing.

"Are you okay, Eric?" John asked quietly.

"I'm fine," Eric replied, though the lie was obvious.

John stayed where he was, arms crossed, silently watching as Eric gripped the desk and twisted the dials one last time.

"Hello?"

Suddenly, a burst of sound tore through the speakers. A rapid and unfamiliar voice spoke in a language Eric couldn't understand.

Eric's breath caught. "Sorry, I don't understand," he stammered. "I speak English if that means anything."

Eric froze as another voice cut through—deeper, deliberate, and marked with a Russian accent.

"Who is this?" the man asked.

John's eyes went wide. He turned and bolted from the room to fetch the others.

Eric swallowed hard. "Uh... who are you?"

"My name is Allistaire Maciej. I was the Russian ambassador to the US. I had just returned to Russia when we lost all communication with the US and Europe. We don't know what happened. Your signal is the first one we've picked up from the United States."

Before Eric could react, another voice broke in, this time with a Chinese accent.

"This is Mao Sī Yǔ. We have intercepted a signal coming from the US. Whoever it is, please respond."

A third voice followed, calm and clipped, with an Indian accent.

"This is Sushil Singh. We, too, have discovered a signal from the US. Has anyone made contact?"

Eric sat frozen as the radio came alive, voices stacking one over the other.

Another chimed in from Japan, then South Korea, then North Korea.

More followed—Taiwan, the Philippines, Bangladesh. Then came Indonesia, Malaysia, Sri Lanka, South Africa, Sudan, Ethiopia, Kenya, and finally, Australia.

One by one, the names rolled in, every new voice another jolt to Eric's chest. They had received the signal. After everything, after days of isolation and despair—they heard him. Eric's heart pounded as the realization settled over him. He could ask for help. He could finally ask for help.

Everyone gathered in the office to see what was going on. They stood wide-eyed and agape as they watched Eric speak into the radio, dozens of accented voices answering him in turn. The impossible was happening—someone out there was listening.

After a pause, Allistaire Maciej's voice came through again, steady and commanding. "And now, it's time for the big question. Who is the person who sent the signal?"

Eric felt the weight of every eye in the room. He took a deep, shuddering breath, his throat tight. "My name is Eric Johansen."

There was an immediate commotion on the line—static mixing with the voices of people reacting across the world. Then Mao Sī Yǔ cut through the noise. "Why did you contact us?"

"Because we need help," Eric said, steadying his voice as best he could. "I don't know why communication has been lost. All I know is that a few days ago, our city experienced a blackout. Our robots are down, and the majority of our population is dead. A lucky few survived, but we require assistance."

Eric's voice cracked as he pushed forward. "There may be others, but we don't know where they are. We have no contact with anyone outside of our city. I fixed an old radio just to reach you. Please—help us rebuild our community."

For a moment, there was only silence. Then the voice from Australia broke through, calm but confused. "What are you talking about?

Everything is fine here. There is no blackout that I know of."

"Yeah, I don't get it," added Sushil Singh. "Everything is fine on our end."

"Same here," came a voice from Kenya.

"Yeah, I'm not sure what you mean," added the voice from the Philippines.

Other voices echoed the same message one by one, the confusion growing until someone finally quieted them all.

"Actually… we think we know what happened," said Mao Sī Yǔ.

Eric leaned closer, his chest tight. "What is it then?" he asked, exhausted from the shouting and tension.

"We just received intelligence from the International Space Station," Mao began. "The Americas, Europe, half of Africa, and all the islands in between… they felt the effects of a solar flare. A coronal mass ejection accompanied the phenomenon—whatever that is."

There was a pause, heavy with what was coming next.

"Apparently… it happened on your side of the planet. In doing so, it wiped out that entire half of the planet—with life, entirely."

Someone in the office gasped. Eric's vision blurred, and he gripped the desk for support as the reality of it crashed over him.

Allistaire Maciej spoke next, his voice softer but resolute. "Our intelligence agency has tracked the signal and pinpointed your location. We will send our forces to help."

"We will too," added Mao Sī Yǔ without hesitation.

There was a pause, and then another voice spoke—this time hesitantly. "I'm not sure if we can send help," said the representative from Indonesia. But we'll try."

"I'll check to see if we can," said another.

"We might as well," came one more.

"We will if we can… but we may be unable to."

Some were willing. Others hesitated, unsure if they could bear the weight of helping. But even those unsure said they would think about it. Eric didn't care who said yes or no. What mattered was that someone was willing to help. That was more than he'd dared hope for.

When the clamor finally quieted, Eric cleared his throat. "Thank you. Thanks for everything."

The voices said their goodbyes one by one. Then the line fell silent, and Eric switched off the radio. He turned to the others. They stood frozen, still in shock that the battered box of knobs had been a working communication device all along.

Arthur broke the silence first. "Eric, why didn't you tell us what the box could do? We could've contacted the other survivors."

"What do you mean?" Eric replied, his voice tired but calm. "You heard them—anyone who isn't dead might not have found a radio."

"That… that thing is a radio?" one of the teenagers asked, wide-eyed.

"Yes. It is," Eric said. "I found it after we got supplies from the stores." He looked around the room, forcing them to meet his eyes. "We need help—all the help we can get. If there are other survivors out there, they'll be thinking the same thing we are. They'll scavenge the warehouses… and eventually, the food will run out."

He exhaled slowly. "What we've got right now was meant to be temporary. We needed to settle, sooner or later. And it turns out… there's no point trying to find new areas outside the city. You heard them. The blackout's not just here—it's nationwide. No… it's the entire West. Taken out."

Everyone was still in disbelief, staring at the dark radio as if it might speak again. Without a word, Eric calmly turned and walked out of the room.

How did they not see? It was their only opportunity for survival, the only path forward. At least now… they had a chance to start fresh.

✳✳✳

After dinner, Eric felt the pull of the night air and slipped outside for some time alone.

He lay down in the dirt, arms spread wide, gazing up at the endless sky. Above him, the stars shimmered—bright, distant, and untouched by everything that had happened. For the first time since the blackout, Eric felt something deep settle in his chest.

Hope.

They had a chance to rebuild, to change things. Somehow, it was all coming together. Tomorrow, he could finally return home. Eric's eyes drifted to the moon, glowing full and soft above the trees. He smiled.

CHAPTER

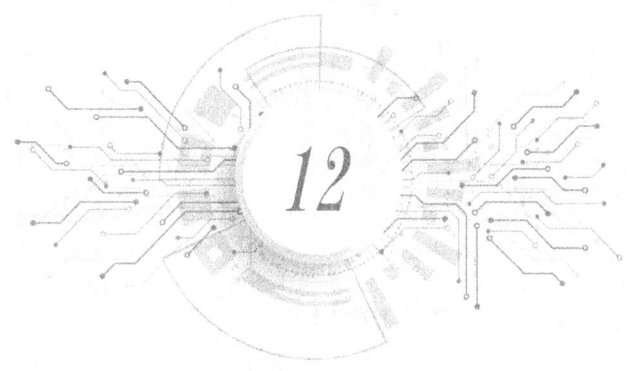

12

E ric was in a forest. The leaf in his hand was smooth against his fingers. A waterfall roared somewhere in the distance. He felt calm and peaceful, which was rare. It was a good feeling—something he hadn't experienced since he took his yearly exams.

A voice called, "Eric?"

Eric responded, "Yes, Dad?"

"Come here; the tour's about to finish."

"Okay."

Eric turned and ran.

The scene changed. He was playing in the park with his friends. It was his turn to go down the slide, but as he did, nausea overwhelmed him. He felt so sick that when he reached the bottom, he threw up on the tanbark. Everyone laughed at him, and one kid called him names. He couldn't stand it, so he kicked the boy in the stomach.

Roger and another AI system told them to stop, but the scenery changed again before he could see what happened.

He had just graduated from business school and was an accountant at a large company whose name he no longer remembered. He was typing at his computer when he heard the fire alarm go off.

Eric jumped from his seat and grabbed his coat. He ran to the elevator and typed the emergency sequence. The elevator carried him down to a floor below the lobby, and when the doors opened, a hoverboard waited. It carried him outside the building, where he saw holes blown through the glass walls.

What person had invaded the building, and why?

Eric jerked awake, his skin clammy with sweat.

It was morning—time to wake up and see what the day would bring.

He went inside to give his report. He told John everything was fine, and nothing had come to attack them.

"Eric, there's a question I've been meaning to ask," John said.

"What is it?"

"Are you sure we're going to return to our own homes after we get help?"

"I'm pretty sure that's what will happen."

"How are we going to be organized? Who will make the laws, and how will we restore the power? Also, where will we go? Someone has to teach the children. Someone has to run the stores. Someone has to manage the bank. How exactly are we going to do this?"

Eric hadn't realized how difficult it would be to organize society again. Almost the entire population was dead—maybe even the president. Who would lead the city? Who would track money or manage stores? And what about goods? Who would cook? Who would make utensils? How would they live again?

"I don't know, John," Eric answered slowly. "I think it's a good idea if we blend with some of the locals. I'm actually thinking of moving to Australia. They're pretty advanced, and I could get a decent job… maybe even help form something to keep us from advancing too fast."

He hesitated, then added, "We have to take these measures soon. If we stay here, we'll perish."

"Eric…"

"Didn't you hear them? Didn't you hear the people on the other side of the world? The country is dead. We're the lucky few who managed to survive. Why simply survive when we have the opportunity to live? There's no hope of restoring the power—it's all dead. We may as well live properly before dying."

"All right, I guess."

Yeah… exactly. All right, thought Eric. They would perish whether they stayed in the country or returned to the city. There was no way of life for them. No one was ready to teach the young or run the stores. They'd be alone. He was right to do what he did.

Eric forced his mind from the distracting anger, remembering the days before the blackout instead. He thought about a time when he could tell Bank he wanted food, and it would appear when he didn't have to lift a finger. But he'd never known what he was missing. Experiencing real trees and birds opened his eyes to how people once lived.

And yet… sadness still lingered. He would never again see anyone from his past. Never again experience the simple joys of his old life. It was hard to accept, but it was the truth. Eric wiped a tear from his face. It was too sad to dwell on. He tried to remember the day of the blackout— what he was doing when it happened—but the memory slipped through his grasp. So much had happened since then that it all felt like a blur. It was only days ago, maybe a week, yet it already seemed like another lifetime.

He *did* remember the chip he'd designed with his team. They had just released it and were making millions in sales. He remembered telling Bank how scared he was of losing his job or his house if anything went wrong. And yet, here he was—with no money, no job, no future… at least, not yet.

Funny, he thought. *I was so scared of that happening, but now I have nothing… and I'm glad. My worst fear came true, but I'm not scared. I feel calm—as if things are finally in order. It's… unusual, but it's true.*

Eric got up and walked to the house. He found John reading a book on the porch.

"What are you reading?" Eric asked.

"An old book," John replied.

"What's it about?"

"Just how to make something called a forge. It explains why it's essential and how we could use it."

"What have you found out?"

"It's nothing major. We just need to find some old metal and melt it into liquid. Then we pour it into a shape and cool it off with water. The people who used to do this were called blacksmiths. They were replaced by robots, though."

"Yeah... I see what you mean."

Eric went inside, a question forming in his head. Humans forging their own weapons? He had never heard that before. What had happened to the human race, once so proactive in discovery, invention, and survival? For the first time, he wondered how many jobs had been replaced with robots.

✳✳✳

After dinner, Eric changed into his nightclothes and lay on the bed. Hopefully, help would arrive the following day. After all, it did take almost a full day to travel.

Things would be better after they received help. They'd go to a new country, blend in, and build their lives again. But what about the issue here—why had they been so unprepared for the blackout in the first place? A disaster of that scale was definitely unexpected, but how had they, as humans, become *this* unprepared?

The answer hit him like a punch to the gut—reliance on technology. AI systems, robots, and machines are doing everything. It caused his downfall. It caused all their downfalls. And if the rest of the world that survived didn't learn that soon… it could fall apart, too.

Eric's head ached. He closed his eyes and fell asleep.

✳✳✳

The next morning, Eric got up and went downstairs. He grabbed a book from the office, and he was in the middle of the second page when he heard an engine roar overhead.

John ran inside and yelled, "Eric, you've got to come see this."

Eric rushed after him and stared up at the sky. "Helicopters and planes," Eric said, breathless with excitement. They watched as a helicopter landed somewhere in the forest. Eric and John chased after it. When they arrived, they saw the door open, and a man in uniform stepped out. Two other men joined him and stood by his side.

"Are you Eric Johansen?" the man asked in an Australian accent.

"Yes," Eric replied.

The man nodded. "We've been dispatched from Australia to transport you there. You can rebuild your lives. Troops from China and Russia will arrive shortly." He paused for a moment, then added, "We'll take you and any survivors to the border protection office, where you'll be granted Australian passports and citizenship—or any citizenship you please. We'll provide you with temporary housing until you can get yourselves some jobs."

Eric sighed. He was going home.

"So… shall we start?"

Eric took a deep breath.

"Yes."

CHAPTER

13

Ten years had passed since the blackout.

The group Eric had led to safety now lived separate lives, though they kept in touch and remained close friends. It amazed Eric how people who were once strangers had become family.

Eric now sat in a brown armchair in his living room, listening to the birds chirping while sipping water from the birdbath he'd built outside some time ago. One might say he'd aged like fine wine, though there were subtle changes. His pale white skin had taken on a slight tan from spending so much time outdoors. Faint, worry lines had begun to form across his forehead. He also wore glasses when reading—his eyesight had weakened over the years—and he wore them now.

So much had happened since that day that his car came to an abrupt halt. The way events had spiraled so far out of the ordinary felt like something pulled straight from an action movie. Eric looked out the window at the clear blue sky, reflecting on everything that had happened ten years ago.

The Australian general had sent John to wake the others. When they all saw the army, they silently rejoiced before gathering their belongings and boarding the aircraft that would take them to Australia, their new home. Arthur, Sabrina, and Sarah stayed behind to work out a few details of their own for a while, but Eric had felt he'd had enough. He already had a plan in mind that he was eager to put into action. So, he and John took the first available helicopter ride and headed straight for the foreign country.

After a day's journey, Eric arrived. He was given clean clothes and a shower and then escorted to the Australian foreign minister's office. There, he was granted citizenship and a new passport and assigned an apartment in a building in Sydney. That was where Eric lived for three years.

During that time, Eric realized mankind's greatest mistake had been relying too heavily on technological advancements. AI systems, hoverboards, and holograms all made people so dependent that no one was prepared for disaster. He had been one of them, and it had cost him everything. But now, he wanted to find a way to warn others not to make the same grave mistake.

He put his plan into motion—but first, he needed a job and money. That part wasn't difficult. With his elite education and experience as a C-suite executive at a world-renowned tech company by the age of twenty-six, Eric quickly found work at another company and climbed back to the top. While he didn't want to rely on technology again, he knew he had to sacrifice that ideology—at least temporarily—to secure his future.

For three years, Eric focused on saving. Still, he made small but meaningful changes. He walked instead of using hoverboards. He never replaced Bank, having sworn off AI systems entirely. Eric planned his own days, scheduled his own rides, and made his own meals. It wasn't easy, but eventually, he got used to it.

He also invested wisely—in stocks and real estate—all calculated moves to grow his wealth. With his business acumen, Eric built his real estate investments into a small company, hiring a manager to run the day-to-day operations.

Next came the most important part of Eric's plan: finding a house like the one where he and the others had once taken shelter. It took time—and a shady deal—but he finally purchased an old, still-functioning house in Daylesford, built in 2018. The purchase included an old pickup truck the desperate former owner threw in practically for free. Eric bought both the house and the truck, resigned from his job, and sold his apartment.

And that was the last time Eric ever set foot in a corporation-owned, self-driving car.

Eric settled into the new house and took to his new life easily. There was a bookshelf packed with books and new skills to learn—like dressing himself, cooking, and even driving the old truck. Shifting gears, pressing pedals… Eric loved it. This life felt more real. But he wanted to do more—the desire to warn people about the dangers of total reliance on technology burned inside him. So, Eric decided to act.

In Daylesford, he met a fellow survivor named Lucas. Together, they founded a nonprofit—dedicated to educating others about those dangers. They gave seminars at schools and libraries, created radio and television programs, and even secured a meeting with the prime minister.

It had been years since the blackout, since the tunnel. Hologram screens and robots now felt like dreams—distant images from another life. Eric wondered if that was how people in the past used to think about the future.

A blue jay flapped its wings overhead, catching Eric's attention as it soared through the sky. It landed gracefully on the edge of a skyscraper, where wild plants now crept up the long-abandoned structure. Eric watched quietly, and for the first time in a while, he truly believed it— hope had returned. They had survived this long, and somehow, they would continue.

Even though Eric sometimes missed his old life, he realized he enjoyed this new existence far more than he'd ever expected. Every day, they discovered things they never would've found within the sterile limits of their old, tech-controlled world. They made their own food, crafted their own tools—things they'd once believed impossible without robots.

It hit Eric then—the jobs robots were known for had all first been done by humans. It was people who figured out how to survive, people who grew tired and passed that labor on to machines. And in doing so, they unknowingly paved the way for their own destruction. His life before the blackout had been ruled by things that didn't truly exist—not in any pure or meaningful way. The walls of technology had confined him. Bank and Amy... they were never alive... just AI systems programmed lines of code that perform their tasks without thought or soul.

Such was the darkness that had corrupted humankind. They gave up freedom for comfort, not realizing that freeing themselves of those unnecessary burdens was the real key to living.

But humans were resilient. They always had been. No matter how far they fell, they never stopped fighting to survive. Their current existence was proof of that resilience. They had created their own destruction—yes—but somehow, they'd risen from the ashes to build something new.

If not all humans, then at least some. Others, no doubt, remained lost—still trapped in the dark, bound by the very creations meant to serve them.

Eric had never thought of his old life that way before, but now he saw it clearly. He had been in the dark, confined by technology. But he'd broken free—along with the other survivors. They'd escaped that prison.

The sun dipped lower, streaking the sky with shades of orange and gold. Eric took one last glance at the horizon and decided he'd like to go for a drive before nightfall. He slipped off his glasses and stood from the armchair, grabbing his keys from the side table. Without another glance back, Eric shut the door behind him and walked to the blue pickup truck parked at the curb.

He slid behind the wheel, started the engine, and shifted into first gear. The old truck rumbled to life. With a small smile, Eric drove down the quiet street, the last rays of sunlight glinting off the hood as he disappeared down the road.

About the Author

Aarkan Singhal is a passionate young writer with a deep interest in the intersection of science, technology, and society. He began writing *Technology: A Ticking Time Bomb* at the age of thirteen, drawing inspiration from visionary dystopian authors such as Ray Bradbury and Neal Shusterman. Despite his age, Aarkan approaches complex themes with striking maturity, using fiction as a lens to examine humanity's growing dependence on technology. In his debut novel, he explores a world brought to its knees by a sudden collapse of technological systems—and the strength of those left to rebuild. Aarkan aims to spark thoughtful dialogue through his work and encourage readers of all ages to reflect on the world around them.